ISBN- 9798402449732

Cover design by: Ezra Rendleman
Library of Congress Control Number: 2021923078
Printed in the United States of America

D1606638

1

Table of Contents

Chapter 1 3

Chapter 2 22

Chapter 3 40

Chapter 4 58

Chapter 5 76

Chapter 6 93

Chapter 7 107

Chapter 8 128

Chapter 9 144

Chapter 10 157

Chapter 11 177

Acknowledgments 198

Chapter 1

I would say it was like any other day, but it was far more exciting. An interstellar probe, *The Sagan*, was returning to the solar system, only the fourth one to do so. Sure, after we discovered Faster-than-Light, or FTL, modules it was possible to send out an automated probe to explore a nearby star system, even if it still took years, and was absurdly expensive, and had a high failure rate. But now we had finally gotten to the point where a return journey was possible.

But this was not just the fourth retuning probe, oh no, *The Sagan* was the first to successfully return from a system with a world with complex life. Previously we had only gathered samples from worlds with simple microbes and single celled organisms. But now we had several soil samples from a biosphere where large multicellular organisms abounded. There were plants like trees, plants like grasses and flowers, animals in the ocean, on the land, and in the air. It had an official designation, but it had been nicknamed *Hortus* after the Latin word for garden, most people stuck with that name.

We had left a few automated rovers behind to survey the planet, and study the native life forms, but the prize we got for now was the soil samples *The Sagan* brought back. While they were just a few of the many samples that it had collected from the system, they were by far the most exciting, and the most interesting.

My name is Dr. Avery Hutton; I was involved in previous studies of microbes brought back from other solar systems, and my name came up when they wanted someone to help lead the analysis of the microbes remotely. I lived on Earth but the microbes were to be analyzed on the space station Randleman in orbit above Earth, once a Zero-G research facility, now a gravity enabled research lab for dangerous potential contaminates. In other words, the perfect place to keep any potentially dangerous microbes that might break out and cause havoc on Earth.

I was not in charge of direct analysis at the lab there, but rather part of mission control on Earth, so even though I would not be directly placing the samples on slides, I was part of this great experiment. The lab was mostly automated; only a few dozen people were there at any one time. One of them was Elia Traub, he was a young astronaut who had taken a position there as his first job. I called him up on vid chat to discuss the project while we waited for the samples to arrive.

"Excited, Elia?" I asked.

"You know it Avery!" he replied.

My job was to walk him through everything. I was very good at biology; he was better at running around in zero-G, even if he and the other people there lived in the rotating section of the station to keep their feet on the floor. He was wearing his standard uniform, full lab coat, with long pants, either blue jeans or in rare cases khakis, this time it was blue jeans. He was technically military, by a very stretched definition, and so sported the standard military buzz cut.

My boss, Dr. Diane Victorovich showed up while we were chatting, she was dressed formally for today, full summer dress still comfortable in Houston weather, "Hey Avery, hi Elia," she said as she walked in with her cup of coffee.

"Good morning Diane," I replied.

"Maybe for you," she said "But the morning doesn't become good until I finish my coffee."

"I have to agree." said Elia.

"Meanwhile you," said Diane to me, "Manage to get by without coffee... HOW?"

"I am pretty sure its magic?" said Elia.

"Anyway" said Diane to Elia, "How is station life treating you?"

"Fine, although I do miss the ability to just go to a restaurant to eat dinner." said Elia taking a sip of coffee himself. "Although I do like the view of stars and flying in zero-G."

"Have you found any girls you like?" asked Diane.

"Ugggh, for the last time, no-. Seriously there are only a few other people here, we are all going to keep it professional" said Elia as he face-palmed.

I saw a smirk on Diane's face.

"Alright" I said while trying to suppress a smirk "we are going to get started on the first experiment right away. As in as soon as *The Sagan* drops it off."

"That's the one to see if *Hortus* microbes like agar plates like the others, right?" said Elia.

"It's always a good first step." I responded, "After all we can't do much without these microbes growing."

"Yeah, that would be a terrible exception to the rule here" said Diane after another sip of coffee.

With every other life supporting planet we have been to, thus far, the life we encountered was not that different from the biochemistry of life on Earth. We always found the same amino acids, familiar base pairs and nucleotides.

This meant that they could also use the same food. Find an alien and they might be able to share a meal with you. Granted we have yet to test out how this works with complex life forms, but for simple life at least, it didn't seem to matter what planet you grew up on. You needed the same stuff, and so could eat the same food as your neighbors on distant planets. So long as it's not toxic to you.

"All we are doing today," began Diane "is moving most of the samples into storage, and getting a few small samples onto Petri dishes to see if they grow on sterile agar plates. We are using a 10 degrees' Celsius difference in temperature for each group, from 10 to 90 degrees Celsius, and we see which group produces the most colonies and go from there once they have baked."

"Assuming that the microbes even survived transport," I said, looking at the schedule. "We did basically dehydrate them so they could be dead by now?"

"Why wouldn't they be alive?" asked Elia, "Every other microbe sample we brought back did just fine, I don't see why our luck should start changing now. Besides Earth microbes can do it. By the way, what are our bets on, fresh new life never seen before, or an old friend?"

"I am going with something familiar," I said. "Remember we already found the Beta Strain in 2 systems. I suspect that this might be a very common occurrence."

"I like your logic" said Diane. "But I will place my odds on it being new; we are over due to discover a new strain of life. Besides we would all get nice job security as the people who figured out the new life strain with the complex ecology."

"My odds" said Elia, "are on it being the specific variety we found twice. I'm going all in double-or-nothing."

We then tried to pass the time. We had to wait for *The Sagan* to arrive at *Randleman* before any of us could do anything. And that wouldn't happen for several more hours. *The Sagan* was still quite a distance away, even twice light speed is slow when you are traveling far enough. Seriously... space is big.

When *The Sagan* finally arrived in the solar system it zeroed in on Earth. Jumping in and out of FTL to "Look around" and see if it was where it thought it was. It dropped out the final time when it was close enough to establish an orbit around Earth. Then it launched its container pod, containing samples from an entire solar system, to *Randleman Station*.

Now for the hard part. Well, hard for the station's staff any way. They had about a (Metric) ton of samples to move onto the station. As we were on Earth, and the task was mostly simple we just waited while Elia and the other moved materials. "Ok," said Elia, "I will go put my suit on."

Then Elia got into a biohazard protection suit, slightly higher pressure than the surrounding air, with a self-contained power/air supply in the backpack that could keep the occupant going for several hours. More convenient than moving around with a hose attached to you, and cheaper as they were made by the same people who manufactured spacesuits. In these days, spacesuits were a necessity, given the number of space stations. Elia came out wearing the suit, into the final air lock. I went through the process of checking him over for any suit damage through the cameras; when I found none I said, "All right you are good to go."

Then began Elia's long day of moving materials through biohazard containment; wheeling heavy carts full of soil samples through the sterile corridors of *Randleman Station*. Or rather watching dozens of robots welling around the containers and occasionally stepping in when one of them had trouble.

Diane left at some point to talk with Dr. Tone Ninsei, the other main person she supervised. We each had a person on *Randleman* to oversee, and she coordinated with us. Suddenly she waved me over.

"Avery," said Diane, "We need you to settle a dispute."

"What kind?" I asked.

"Do we need to look into type first or their survivability on Earth?" said Tone.

"Why don't we do both at once?" I asked.

"Because they both require the whole incubator to get enough to do a test, and only one is working."

"I would go with testing type first." I said, "That will affect our experiments going forward, right?"

"Told you?" said Diane.

"Alright," said Tone, "Scheduling it up. But don't blame me if it gets out and we find out it can live on Earth."

"Given how close to Earth *Hortus* is environmentally I would not be surprised if that did happen." I said. I caught a glimpse of Tone's T shirt for today, this one had "Don't Panic" printed on in in bright red letters. I rolled my eyes at him then returned to my desk.

"Ah... we have a problem," said Elia. "One of the bots crashed, and we have to re-work the system."

"Do you need help?" I asked.

"Nah, I got it." said Elia.

Eventually they finally emptied the ship.

"Ok," said Elia. "Now we just got to set up the Petri Dishes?"

"Yeah" I said, "Make sure the machine uses a new spoon for each one."

"Right, right" said Elia. He then set the lab to move the materials onto five Petri dishes, close them, and put them in the incubator set for 10 degrees Celsius. Then the lab repeated the process 8 times for the other incubators, each one set 10 degrees higher than the previous one, and then all was done.

"Right, now what?" said Elia.

"That's everything," I said, "time for you call it a day."

"Alright," said Elia as he got up to go through decontamination and then get some dinner from the station cafeteria. Then with my job done, I got up to go home. As I got ready to go, I saw Diane pack up and talk to Tone.

"Ok I am leaving," she said, "Don't stay too late."

"I just need to catch up on a few things," said Tone, "Don't worry."

The next day Diane and I arrived to find Tone already there.

"Did you get here before me?" I asked.

"I never left," he said, "I got carried away."

"I... I told you to go home last night," said Diane now suddenly behind me. "Now you are making me look bad for going home... it's too early for this... let me get my coffee so I can understand what happened."

Then we got to work, and I surveyed the experiment.

"Hey Diane," I said, "We have good news."

"The samples grew?" she asked perking up.

"Yep," I said.

"We won't know for sure until analysis is complete," said Elia. "But first glance tells me they might do very well at 50 degrees."

"We can do that once we have counted the colonies in each dish," said Diane.

After the computer counted all the colonies, in all the dishes, we had our answer. They grew best at about 50 degrees C, and that result was statistically significant. So now we had a way to keep growing the colonies.

"Ok," said Elia, "Microbes are behaving well, and we can grow them fairly well; now what boss?"

14

"Now we have to see if this is one we have seen before, or if it is new," I adjusted my seat. "Each strain we have encountered thus far has its own language of DNA, as well as a few tell tail indicators. Time to look for them."

I then helped Elia go through the set-up process; I have a PhD, but I'm not qualified as an astronaut like he was. And he was Biohazard level 4 qualified, so he could do anything we needed him to. So, we set up the various experiments that would cook overnight to determine if we knew the strain.

The next day we found out that these were "Beta Strain"; a form of life we had seen two times previously, well now three times. We had never encountered any viruses for this strain of life, which was strange, we would have thought that they would have evolved those as well.

Diane shared a concern with me over lunch.

"We have now seen Beta Strain life three times out of the five cases where we analyzed life for other planets; why?" asked Diane.

"Maybe we just got a fluke?" I reply.

"Yeah, but, I would have thought, if panspermia is really possible, which this suggests, why have we only seen this one repeat; what is special about it? Is anything special about this?"

In panspermia she meant a process in which organisms might be able to move from one planet to another planet naturally. It was suspected, up until Mars, and everything else we once thought might house life in the solar system turned out to be really truly dead, that life on Earth might have originated elsewhere in the solar system, then hitchhiked to Earth on a meteor. With this being the third encounter of Beta Strain life, well... we were talking about something a bit more ambitious than just inter planetary panspermia.

"It's like flipping a coin 10 times," I said taking a bite out of my sandwich, "If you flip a coin 10 times you might get 10 heads, does that mean if you flip it an 11th time, you will get another head?"

"No," said Diane "The odds are still 50-50. The previous flips don't matter."

"We have 5 samples; how many stars are there in the galaxy again?"

"I don't know, billions."

"And how many planets that might have life?" I asked.

"Probably an ungodly huge number."

"So, is five a significant sample size?"

"I know, I know," said Diane palming her forehead, "I know it's stupid but I can't help but feel like this might mean something. I … maybe, I don't know, maybe I am just worrying because they decided to relax the protocols on us, I just feel like something is wrong."

She was talking about how, about a year ago, the Global Space Exploration Alliance, commonly called G.S.E.A, had decided that some of the safety protocols were unnecessary and they decided to do away with some of them. Particularly in regard to some of the more expensive equipment.

"Like what?" asked Tone.

"I don't know, um, do you ever get a sinking feeling?" said Diane as she took a bite of her lunch and continued, "Like something horrible is about to happen and there is no way to stop it?"

"Yeah, every now and then," I said, "Normally it means nothing and I am just nervous."

"Well," said Diane, "I have that feeling now, and it's a lot worse than what I am used to. The rational part of my brain is sure it means nothing- After all Global Space Exploration Alliance is confident that everything will be OK, hence the relaxed protocols. So, it could just be that I am just being paranoid, and that my paranoia has latched onto something of no consequence and it all means nothing."

"But?" I asked.

With a deep sigh Diane responded "I feel like, I don't know. Like this time is somehow different, I mean we are more worried about pathogens because of the complex life on *Hortus*, but the scientists are safe, right?"

Now I began to understand her fear. We were always concerned with pathogens, but we had never found any pathogenic microbes before. Earth microbes generally seemed to outcompete any alien microbes in an Earth like environment, even beta strain. But now, for the first time we had microbes from a truly Earth like environment, not just trace amounts of oxygen but a real oxygen rich atmosphere, with large organisms which it might be worthwhile to infect.

We had some concerns that this might be the first time we came across life that could be a serious threat to life on Earth, it was different this time. With the relaxed protocols it might actually happen. We couldn't be sure but these *Hortus* microbes had a shot of being correctly adapted to thrive and even outcompete earth life. We had raised our concern's but there was not a lot that could be done, management was pushing for discoveries. Discoveries meant funding and public support, with which we could do more exploration.

"You're worried management has gotten complacent?" I asked "And this will be the one time it matters?"

Diane nodded.

"Also, the Beta Strain does appear to be particularly tough," added Tone.

I nodded in agreement. It took an insane amount of effort to kill Beta Strain microbes. They just don't seem to care, still active in environments where comparable Earth microbes might try to escape with suspended animation. They survived in suspended animation where Earth microbes, or the microbes of the other strains we found, died.

Our antibiotics don't do the trick, at least not to the point where someone infected would die from the medicine before the disease started to be affected. So, if there was a pathogenic Beta microbe, then anyone who caught it, would simply have to hope their immune system was able to handle it. Given that this pathogen was completely unknown to our immune system, not exactly spectacular odds. Previously this had not meant anything, no one had gotten hurt. Nothing we had found, could survive oxygen, even Beta strain microbes were outcompeted by Earth microbes, so long as the environment they were fighting over resembled Earth. Hortus was practically identical to Earth in every way that mattered to microbes. All other things being equal, Beta strain was just too strong.

Chapter 2

The first time Elia called me on a day off I was worried that something was wrong. Now I know it was probably because he just wanted to chat.

"Lonely again up there?" I asked.

"Not really," said Elia, now in a plain T shirt. "I kind of like having only a few people to worry about, not really a fan of social drama."

"No one is, except when it happens to fictional characters."

"True." Elia paused to reflect, "Actually this is probably the happiest I have ever been."

"Seriously?"

"Yep," said Elia. "D... Don't get me wrong, I have had a good life, but, now I finally feel worth something. I mean I am part of a mission to explore nearby stars, on behalf of all of Earth. Something that a hundred or two hundred years ago was all science fiction, impossible."

At this point a cat jumped up onto Elia's shoulder.

"When did you get a cat?" I asked.

"Oh, she is not mine, we banded together to get a mascot up here."

The cat meowed at Elia who picked her up to start petting her.

"Does she have a name?" I asked.

"Her name is Sara," said Elia, scratching Sara's ears.

"She is cute," I said.

"And fits better on a small space station than a dog ever would, also may be good against any escaped rats." said Elia.

"There are no escaped rats," I said.

"See, she is already doing a great job," said Elia.

"Any way." I said trying not to roll my eyes, "What were you saying about impossible."

"Oh," said Elia. "Any way in old science fiction they used to have people who live lives a bit like ours. Sure, we can't go on a day trip to Alpha Centauri yet, but otherwise we are living a dream that some might have called impossible."

"How so?" I asked

"Well, war used to be a thing that affected many people's lives," said Elia.

"By affect, do you mean end?" I asked.

"Yes, other things were infections, starvation, not enough money... but they often dreamed of a future time where all these things would be gone. No war, everyone coexists peacefully, everyone has the medicine they need, to them it seemed like an impossible dream."

"And yet here we are," I said leaning back in my chair. "Not exactly far off from the old dreams?"

"Yeah, I like to keep the fact that I am living a life people would kill for in the past to be a good way to keep things in perspective you know," said Elia. "I know we have problems in our society, and I hope we can fix them but, well, 100 years ago people starved to death because they could not afford food, now that's almost unheard of, things have been and still are getting better."

Sara meowed to that.

"We still have time to screw it up," I said. "After all sometimes things go sour, and as you said things aren't perfect. After all we still have holdouts from various nations that got absorbed into the Global Republic."

"Maybe," Elia adjusted his seat, "But you should know better than to be too much of a pessimist, given your profession."

"Yeah I guess," I replied. "The world has become a more and more wonderful place over the past few decades." I thought about something and then had to ask "What are you doing up there, on your days off?"

"Eh, mostly I just relax," said Elia. "We have some chores to do, but keeping track of the experiments only takes so much time, especially when all we are doing is maintenance and making sure the little samples don't die."

"I had never really thought about that, you're up there all day every day for how long?" I asked.

"Another 6 months," came the reply. "But I already signed up for another year after that."

"Wow," I said "I would have gone mad by now."

"Eh, I like the peace and quiet," Elia reclined in his seat and continued, "besides I will take a long vacation in between, get all peopled out and visit my family, you know."

"I see." I said, "What are you planning?"

"Two months of travel, visiting most of my friends and family, and a few places I always wanted to visit as well," said Elia looking at the ceiling. "Actually, maybe you and/or Diane could come visit me on my vacation then."

"Really?" I asked scratching my head.

"Of course, you are both great long-distance co-workers, maybe you could both come visit my family."

"I'll think about it," I said as Sara ran off.

"That's what Diane said too. Looking forward to your conference next week?"

"Yep, I am still making last minute adjustment to my schedule," I said. "And practicing going through my speech so I know what I am doing."

"Well, be sure to tell me how you did when you give your little speech."

"I will, have a great day and see you tomorrow."

"You too buddy, bye," Elia then closed the vid chat.

My attention then turned to Robey, my Phi-d0 model robotic dog. He was just waking up and removing himself from his recharge station. He barked good morning and I took him outside to play fetch.

Theoretically I didn't have to play fetch, but it was fun. That was the appeal of robotic dogs. Don't need to be let outside or taken on walks, or fed or provided water. Not likely to bite or get fleas. Just give them a recharge station connected to a power outlet and for the most part they take care of themselves. Not only that but there are many places that don't allow pets, that make exceptions for robotic ones. All this was taken into account when I asked mom for a dog when I was 5 and she suggested a robotic one.

When playing fetch, I started to see that he was getting slow, which brought up another advantage. I could get Robey a new body fairly easily. Just transfer his program and memories over and good as new. No need to mourn, just upgrade.

Eventually Robey got tired, mostly because his motors overheated, and we went back inside. It was time for me to relax a bit, and watch some TV.

Later in the weekend Tone called back. He had some concerns to share over lunch. Today his shirt said "Hello from the otter slide" and showed the image of several otters on a slide.

"This is a Beta Strain microbe, incredibly tough, now over Earth," he said. "If it breaks out onto Earth how much trouble do you think we are in?"

"We would be in deep trouble," I said. "But it's not going to happen." I took a bite of food before responding. "They have quarantine procedure for a reason; as long as we follow that, everything will be ok. Even if it does break out onto the station, it's in orbit, we can incinerate any biological matter leaving for Earth. Not even Beta Strain life can survive a plasma furnace."

"Yes, but," said Tone, "They relaxed the safety protocols because the last two runs went well, and we have not found anything pathogenic before; what happens if these relaxed protocols don't do the trick?"

"Then it breaks out onto the station, medical teams are sent in, and they revert to full Biohazard 4 procedure," I said. "Just because they relaxed the protocol for *Randleman* doesn't mean they can't get it back up to the old standards. It still fulfills those requirements."

"Still, then anyone on *Randleman* is in trouble," said Tone.

"Yes but," I said, "Not dead, we could still save them. That is what the medical teams are for. Is there an antibiotic agent that will kill Beta Strain microbes that would not kill the human host? No, at least not that we know of. But bed rest, food, and maybe some quick thinking could still do the trick. We would also know better than to lower the protocols again."

"So, what?" asked Tone, "It's basically hope for the best?"

"Even then worse case, we cremate the bodies via plasma furnace." I said "Yes it would be sad, yes it would be tragic, but we would learn from it. This is like the lesson of the Titanic."

"What?" asked Tone, "Look out for icebergs?"

"Also have enough life boats for everyone, and make sure that every boat can talk to one another."

However, by the middle of the next week there had been a snag. First, on Monday there was an accident in one of the labs. One of the samples from *Hortus* was dropped on the ground and the container broke. Initially we believed the spill was contained, but some of it must have been missed. We never figured out how exactly but perhaps some of the seals that should have kept any biological agent contained weren't examined as well as they should have been. Or maybe we did not sterilize everything as much as we should have. Personally I think the protocols and procedures we had should never have been relaxed. Though I admit it might have been somewhat inevitable, perhaps it doesn't matter. On Tuesday someone reported being sick, by Wednesday they had specialized doctors on board and, as far as they could tell, everyone on the station was infected.

"You sure it will be fine?" asked Diane.

"No" I said honestly, "But I don't want everyone on *Randleman* thinking that they are dead. So, I am going to say everything is fine and hope for the best."

Diane simply nodded.

I knew she had several people to keep track of up there, but she and Elia went way back.

As she wandered away to worry about someone else, Elia came back to the screen.

"They say it looks like some sort of bacterial infection, they don't see any symptoms that look exactly like anything we keep up here, so we are all hoping it's just going to be a minor fever."

"So just an ordinary Earth microbe, take a few weeks off, round of antibiotics, everyone is fine?" I asked.

"We hope," said Elia, "They are doing blood tests so hopefully we will know soon."

Any hope remaining that this would be simple was dashed when they got the results back. The specialized doctors who responded when a biohazard space station had an alert, ran their tests and got the result of Beta Strain Microbes.

"So, in other words, I am among the first people to get an alien cold?" asked Elia.

"Looks like it" said the doctor, "Here is your treatment regimen, for goodness sake don't stop it even when you feel better, the last thing we need is an alien pathogen that is also resistant."

In a few days, everyone would feel better, sure they still had to go through the entire antibiotic regiment, but, of course, there was a catch. A catch that Elia and I saw immediately.

"Doctor, you and I both know that Beta Strain is already immune to Earth antibiotics," whispered Elia.

Beta strain was tough, much tougher than Earth strain. No poison or antibiotic would kill it, not without killing everything else we had encountered first. Humans included.

"Yeah," said the doctor quietly, "Don't tell anyone else, and try to hope for the best. Look we will find something, just try to get some rest."

"Yes ma'am" said Elia without another complaint and took the first pill. "Might as well keep up the illusion, right?" he whispered to me.

In all likelihood, it was a sugar pill anyway, or maybe was medicine that just was not an antibiotic.

The director of the Global Health Alliance (GHA), Dr. Jane Foster, came down to our office to give us a little speech.

"Don't tell anyone outside of the Global Space Exploration Alliance, or the Global Health Alliance, about what happened, or is happening. If you can try to provide moral support to everyone up there, if you have any idea about how to fix this, email me directly. I promise you we will get through this. If anyone asks, tell them we are giving them antibiotics. We are not, but we can still try to convince them that they are and that it will work"

Our Global Space Exploration Alliance (G.S.E.A) boss, Larry Fox, stood by her the entire time. Then began the real challenge of the day, debating if there was any way to fix this, while also keeping a strong face.

I was sitting at a table with some of my colleagues and we went back and forth all day. Antibiotics didn't work, there was no known substance that was more toxic to Beta Strain life than Earth life. No way that we knew of to hinder their growth, or filter it out of the system.

"I am not sure if there is anything we can do," said Dr. Charles Walter, "Other than just tell them it will get better."

"I know, I know," I said, "But it's hard to be optimistic."

"Well, I don't know, these pathogens have never seen a human immune system before, maybe they don't know what to expect?" said Charlie.

"Well I suppose that's as optimistic as we can get." I said feeling exhausted "Wait, what if we boosted the immune system?"

"I don't know." Charlie took a sip of tea, "Someone probably already thought of that... But if everyone thought that then, ohhh, they might not tell anyone else. Maybe we shouldn't think that they already thought of..."

"I am going to email Dr. Foster," I said, "And ask her about that."

"Ok, good let me know how it turns out," said Charlie.

I wrote a short email, "I am sure you have already thought of this, but what about immune system boosters?"

I got my reply within a few minutes. "Yep, that is something we are trying, but thanks anyway, I would hate for someone to think, 'Eh they probably already tried that' when we haven't and it could save the day."

When chatting with Elia later I asked, "So how are you feeling?"

"Ok for now, but, I don't know, it feels like today might be the last day I ever feel fine for a while, if not forever," he replied.

"I am sure you will be fine in a few weeks," I said, putting on a brave face.

"Yeah, as soon as they figure out which treatment works," said Elia. "They got everyone on a different set of regimens, I think that they are experimenting to see who has the first positive result. Did you give them any ideas"?

"I suggested immune system boosters but they said they were already trying that," I replied.

"Eh, could be worse. I mean I might think differently in a few days."

"It might not even last that long. I mean these microbes have never seen a human immune system, they probably don't know how to fight it."

"Or they might have dealt with immune systems like ours on *Hortus* in which case, I'm the one who's in trouble."

The first few days, nothing happened, at least not on the surface. The daily blood tests showed more and more of the pathogen. No one said anything though, the last thing we wanted was for anyone to give up. Then, well, everyone on the station, began to feel worse. The emergency doctors were fine, they were in biohazard gear from day one and often worked through robots, so that was good. But all their patients were dying. Fever and coughing seemed to be the early symptoms. Then pneumonia set in. About a week after the first person was infected we had our first death of this Beta Strain disease.

It was Sara. We held a small service for her with the crew. Comments like, 'she was such a cute kitty', were common. As well as worries about everyone else.

Then as the days went by, more people got worse.

"So, I heard about what happened up there," I said to Elia.

Elia was coughing, "I don't... I don't think I will last much longer up here either," he said over the line.

"Don't say that, try and stay positive. I mean, they have some more ideas," I lied.

"Ok, Avery, I am positive... I'm positive that I am going to die today."

"Well...," I was interrupted by a coughing fit, and then when Elia grabbed a bucket, I could see him coughing up blood.

"I... I'm sure...," I couldn't think of anything positive to say. Five people had already died, no one showed any signs of recovery. Worst of all, Elia was already at the state that earlier patients had reached just hours before death.

"Well don't let me keep you too long," said Elia.

"Your dyi... you're sick, wouldn't you rather have the company?"

Elia had another coughing fit, "You and I both know I am not going to make it that long; I won't keep you away from your work." He coughed up another storm.

"Just one little favor? Please?" he asked.

"Anything."

"Could you stay on the line, while I call my mom?"

I am not sure what was hardest, watching Ms. Traub seeing her son die, or watching my friend die. I am going to go with both. Eventually Diane, and anyone who knew Elia at all was on the line. Every coworker, every class mate, every random friend. When we saw him sign a DNR form I cried, everyone cried. We all stayed online in any way we could. One of the doctors stood by him in a biohazard suit. Eventually Elia was pale. He looked like he had several rashes and had blood trickling out of his nose. Somehow, he was moved, as it by some unknown force, to give a little speech to us, wheezing and hacking as he talked.

"I…I know this is hard, but I knew this was a risk, it always…" he gasped for air, "It was always worth it for me, and even knowing that this is how it ends, I would do it all over again, in a heartbeat. I feel like I am part of something greater than myself, that one day this … (HACK), this will have been worth it, one day in the future, someone will step out onto a planet under an alien sun. I feel like something we learned here today, will have made it worth it. Thank you for being here, and know that I die, doing what I loved, and that in my mind, it was worth it." He then closed his eyes and tried to fall asleep.

A few hours later Elia suffered another bout of coughing, after that he asked the doctor, "Could you take this mask off please?"

Once the oxygen mask was off, Elia said, "Thank you." And he closed his eyes for the last time.

Chapter 3

After Elia's death I couldn't handle it; as soon as I could I went home and called mom though the computer.

"Mom?" I said fighting though tears.

"Oh dear, are you ok?"

"Yeah," I forced out, "But, but..."

"You said that there was a problem, did something go wrong?" she asked.

I nodded.

"I am sorry honey," said mom. "There was a news report... was it the space station with the people who were infected by an alien microbe?"

"Um... yes... when did they go public?" I asked.

"Just today," said mom, "Look, I know that you probably can't talk about it... but if you need anything I am here... ok?"

"Ok... thanks mom." I said "Talk to you tomorrow?"

"Of course," said Mom then she canceled the call.

Robey approached me and nuzzled my leg. I looked down at him and he whined at me.

"It's ok Robey," I said. "Daddy is just upset because a friend died." I picked him up.

Robey looked up at me with his camera eyes. They were rather big, puppy like, and made him cute, in a weird robotic way. I sighed and began robo-puppy therapy.

I didn't eat much that day.

A few days later, after the last infected person on *Randleman* passed away, we began planning for the deceased. The analysis of the samples from *Hortus* were put on hold while we tried to sort things out. On one hand, we were still mourning and we had a duty to the dead and to bring back their remains to Earth. As much as that was true, we also had to figure out how and why it happened, as well as how we would proceed, or if we would at all. No one had ever died of an alien infection before, so we had to record what we knew.

While cleanup crews scrubbed the station up and down before they irradiated the interior, we got news about the autopsy reports.

The Chief Medical examiner, Dr. Gordon Hurt began on vid com, still in a biohazard suit, "So far we have identified 24 separate species of pathogen, and some of them seem to be able to navigate a human body fairly well. Apparently, our physiology is similar enough to their native hosts that they can infect us without much trouble."

"Is there any one pathogen that stands out, does the most damage?" I asked.

"The one we have found most frequently," said Dr. Hurt, "is what we are tentatively calling Pathogen Six. It seems to infect the respiratory system and ultimately causes pneumonia; if that does not kill you, it continues damaging the lungs until they tear when you try to breath. We believe it may be airborne."

"How many people did Pathogen Six kill?" asked someone.

"So far, over half of the deceased," said Dr. Hurt. "Many of the rest died from secondary infection; some of the other Beta Strain pathogens managed to destroy the immune system. It's possible that these pathogens simply took anything that our bodies could throw at them. These microbes are unlike anything I've ever seen."

"So, there is nothing that can be done once you're infected?" asked Diane, "And the harder you fight, the quicker you die?"

"We are still looking into it," said Dr. Hurt, "but, if anyone else gets infected, the most we can realistically do is try to keep them comfortable while they die. As for fighting back, it doesn't seem to matter; the people we gave immune supplements to did not die any sooner or later. Any more questions?"

No one had any.

"Thank you, Dr. Hurt," said Dr. Foster, "Call us if you have any developments."

Everyone else then left the room; I had to discuss funeral plans with Diane.

"They are doing the funeral for Elia in two weeks," I said.

"Yeah, I have three funerals I'm invited to," she replied. "I might not be able to make it to Elia's; I have the other two at the same time."

"Oh well, I can explain why you are not there; after the conference is over next week, I will travel out to his folks' place."

"You're still going to the conference? The one about space exploration where you are scheduled to speak?" she asked, scratching her head.

"If I can... I should have enough time to do that and Elia's funeral, but I have already canceled my presentation."

"Can't go through with it now?"

"Not right now, maybe in a year or two, but for now I don't think I am in the best position to ... well... do much."

"Fair enough," Diane took a sip of her coffee, "Every family is doing a different thing."

"Yeah", I said, "I know Tabatha asked to be double cremated."

"I hear Jeff asked to be launched into Jupiter," said Diane.

"Elia went with cremation," I said, "Wanted his ashes spread in Hawaii because he always wanted to go there."

"Do you think that's smart?" asked Diane, "After all this was a nasty plague, and if it gets out…"

"They've already tested that," I said, "Turns out you can kill it with fire, or at least a plasma furnace."

"I know, I know, I am just worried someone will do something stupid," said Diane, "Like try to bring the whole body back to be buried."

"I don't think anyone would ever be that dumb," I said.

Watching the news later that day was depressing, in part because the deaths of my colleagues filled almost all of it. If there was any happy news it was buried under the stories of the dead. However, the worst part of all was when Diane's fears turned out to be justified.

"Today a legal battle begins as the family of Nicole Turner, one of the many scientists who died due to the alien microbes from *Hortus,* battles against the UNHO for legal rights to bury their daughter the way they wish to," said Eric Long, a reporter for WWN.

Ms. Turner, the mother of Nicole, then spoke on screen wearing way too much makeup, "My daughter just died, and they have the gall to tell me how to bury her, how to mourn her. No, we will care for her our way, not the way some soulless government bureaucrat wants us to burn her, but according to our tradition."

"Which is what?" asked Long.

"Our family does not believe in cremation," said Ms. Turner, "It is our belief that everyone, including my daughter, should be buried whole. They have already desecrated her corpse enough with their autopsy. Now they want to burn her? No, I want my daughter's remains to be on view at her funeral. And I want to at least bury my daughter according to tradition."

All I could think of was, "OH MY GOD THIS WOMAN IS GOING TO GET HERSELF AND EVERYONE ELSE KILLED."

The news cast continued, "We asked the GHA their take on the matter. Dr. Jane Foster had this to say.

"We respect that Ms. Nicole Turner is dead, and we respect that her family has a right to mourn, but she has to be cremated due to safety concerns," said Dr. Foster. "The pathogens that killed her are still alive. If we cremate her, we can guarantee that none of the pathogens will survive; if we can't do that then more people will die. I sympathize but there is no way to safely return Nicole's body to Earth and to her family, without cremation."

Eric returned to the screen "The Turner family follows the Eastern Orthodox faith, which expressly forbids cremation. For now, it has been ordered by the government to put any cremation of Nicole on hold until a decision can be reached, back to you."

I decided to check the internet, and a few short hours later, it had taken a side, specifically Ms. Turner's side. Social media had turned Dr. Foster into an insane scientist who when asked "Why can't the Turners bury their daughter?" responded "We can't do that." Anyone who pointed out that the quote was hideously out of context was torn apart. The next day this newscast happened.

"I never said that Ms. Turner could not bury her daughter," said Dr. Foster, "I only said that we have no choice but to cremate her body."

"And who gave you the right to do that?" asked Anna Bailey, another reporter.

"It's not that. It's about safety. If even a single *Hortus* microbe from her corpse got out, it could mean the end of all life on Earth. We all saw what it can do. Do you think that it will magically go away just because she is dead? We have to dispose of her body properly; I am sorry but those are the facts. If we release her body as it is, we risk every single person on Earth, possibly in the solar system. We can't do that."

"It can't be that dangerous," said Anna. "Diseases were something that killed our ancestors, not something we deal with today."

Dr. Foster sighed, "If we could fight it, we could have saved Nicole. Don't you think we would have done that if we could?"

"Are you saying you're incompetent?"

"No, I'm saying that these pathogens can't be dealt with by modern medicine, and we have no more ways of stopping a Beta Strain infection today, than we did when Nicole got infected."

"What about alternative medicine?" Anna asked, raising an eyebrow.

"Aside from the fact that most 'alternatives' are untested, we decided to try many of them. We tried almost everything we could think of. Anything that anyone could think of, no matter how crazy it looked. We did everything short of poisoning Ms. Turner and her colleagues if we thought it might help. Absolutely nothing worked." Dr. Foster pressed her palms against her forehead. "When I say we have nothing, I mean we have no idea in the slightest how, or if, we can deal with it. Right now, destroying Ms. Turner's remains is the only way to be sure that an infection will not break out."

"So, the Turner family can't mourn because an infection MIGHT break out?" asked Anna with crossed arms.

"Do any of you have any idea how dangerous this infection is?" asked Dr. Foster, "It has already killed dozens of people; there were already concerns about releasing the ashes of the deceased. We can't simply release her corpse as is. An infection WILL break out and more people will die."

Not many people took our side in the story. They didn't fear the consequences of an outbreak; it simply was not that scary to them. It was the unfortunate unexpected downside to near perfect global health; sickness became a lot less scary.

The conversation came up at lunch the next day.

"So, I was wrong, people really are that stupid," I said to Diane.

"I have never been more disappointed to have been right," said Diane who in a startling turn of events was drinking coffee, and also looked like she got up five minutes ago and threw on sweatpants.

I took a sip of my water.

"What is going on?" asked Tone, whose shirt contained a pun so awful I refuse to repeat it here.

"Don't you watch the news? Or pay attention to social media?" I asked.

"No why?"

"Someone wants to bring one of the bodies back to Earth, pre-cremation," Diane sighed.

"Oh… well I don't think that could actually happen, I mean come on, that would be crazy," said Tone.

Suddenly Director Larry Fox made an announcement, "There has been a change of plans-everyone. They are actually releasing Ms. Turner's body."

In my shock, I spit my water everywhere, including Diane's face.

"Sorry," I whispered.

"It's ok," she responded. "If I had been drinking it would have been mutual."

Director Fox continued, "Also Dr. Foster wants to preemptively activate the Omega Protocol, and move everyone who worked with Beta Strain to a secure biohazards response facility. Which means that many of you should probably go home and pack, you will be officially emailed shortly if not already. Thank you."

I checked my email; so, did Diane and Tone. "Got to pack too?" I asked.

"Yep," said Diane still wiping my water off her face.

"Me too," said Tone.

"Well, I guess I better get going." I said.

"Me too.," said Diane. "See you on Failsafe."

I went home and started packing. The Omega Protocol was a way to quickly get people deemed to be "important" to a safe location where they can sort out whatever emergency is going on. It also allowed for pets, and some family members to come with each "important" person. All the forms were filled out in advance, you, any spouse and children you might have, and a plus one. In my case the only mark was for Robey, who saw I was packing and went into his crate.

While you could take some people with you, extended family and friends were usually out. You might be able to take a significant other, even if you are not legally married, but you could not bring your parents, or siblings, barring special circumstance. Thus, my mom had to stay on Earth, as well as Tone's and Diane's parents. Tone was particularly worried, as his folks were not always the most... concerned with diseases.

Nevertheless, we were off to the Global Republic Failsafe station, you could call it another research space station. But where *Randleman Station* was relatively small, this was several kilometers of rotating station. Safe from any emergencies on the ground, we could respond to the situation in safety. It had the capacity to recycle air and water as long as the equipment held together and it had power. Like most stations it had a Fusion reactor, it also had solar panels which could gather power as long as the sun was shining. It even came with its own recycling plant; fuel refinery and its onboard farms could provide food for a million people, and it was about to do just that. So, we were all set to respond to a breakout if it happened, or near anything really. If all else failed, the station was built to wait it out. We could last for years, maybe even decades with some work, and then act as a last bastion of Humanity if all else should fail.

But self-sustaining infrastructure was just one of its abilities. It contained dozens of labs, each stocked full of high-tech equipment. Including labs up to biohazard level 4. It had its own breeding colony of lab rats, and the personnel and equipment to maintain them. There were quarantine zones if anyone was maybe infected. Shuttles were included and the resources to maintain them for years. There was even its own rather large supply of environmental suits, ranging from vacuum suits, to diving suits, to yes, biohazard suits.

The entire station was designed for two things: One, if the apocalypse ever came, it could function as the base of operations for those trying to save the world. Two, serve as the place where some of humanity might survive to rule the Earth again another day.

The rotating area that we would spend most of our time was divided into seven sections. One and two were where most of the living spaces were located. And they contained room and amenities for children, pets, adults, and recreational spaces for everyone. Two also contained the infirmary for anything short of biohazard level four. Three contained most of the offices for the bureaucrats and managers, as well as some room for storage. Section four contained the hydroponic farms that provided the station with air and food, although we could only get meat from the stored supplies. Five and six were the main labs. And seven was an emergency section; if something happened to the others, be it minor damage to the school or total destruction of the rest of the station, seven could take over. It contained some of everything, though not as good, it would be good enough. Seven also had the quarantine zones.

The non-rotating portion was mostly for docking and some storage. From it, shuttles could be launched. We could get anywhere on Earth in a few hours, and back just as quickly, which was good as the infection looked ready to start in Chile, which was Nicole Turner's burial site. It had been one of her favorite places to visit, so her family chose it as her final resting place.

I visited Diane and her family on board; she was not legally married yet, but she put David down as her plus one, and her young son Olli, came as immediate family. She also brought a dog who was currently barking at me from under a couch.

"Hey Avery," she said, "Don't worry about our dog Lady, she doesn't bite."

"My first clue as to that was that she is hiding from me," I said.

"Hey buddy," said David, "How is the single life treating you?"

"Good," I said, "How is the all but married life treating you?"

"We are fine, though Olli is scared," said Diane.

To be fair, their son Olli was only four; also I was scared.

I then noticed that Tone was also there.

"Huh, you too, Tone? I asked.

"Well we would normally still be on the clock," he said, then there was silence as everyone thought about why we were here.

"Up for a game of scrabble?" asked Tone.

I felt the weight on my shoulders lessen "Sure," I said and we played a few rounds. We tried to have fun...

but with disaster looming, it was hard to relax... even if I knew it would be my last chance for a while.

Chapter 4

I had been living at the Failsafe station for only 1 week when we got word that the Beta Pathogen had broken out, from the Turner funeral, because of course it did. I was not surprised, but I was very upset. This was what might be the beginning of a terrible scenario. Dr. Foster addressed the concerned public.

"The GHA will, of course, do everything in its power to contain this disaster, and attempt to curtail it as soon as we can. But we cannot guarantee that our response will be able to help everyone, or indeed anyone at this point," said Dr. Foster. "We will of course keep you informed of any and every development."

"She is a strong woman," said Diane.

"Yeah, in her shoes I would have said 'I TOLD YOU SO!' by now," I said.

"Amen to that," said Tone, drinking a cup of tea, while wearing a shirt that had a horse spewing a rainbow out of its mouth.

The station's director, a well-dressed man named Dr. Ivan Soukup, made an announcement over the intercom.

"Ladies and gentlemen, I am sure you by now have heard that we are enacting full quarantine procedure; we have the ability to grow food and recycle air and water, but we will be limited in our diet once the current food supply is expended."

Which is to say, we have an unlimited supply of tofu and salad; it has everything you need to survive, even if you would rather have some meat. But don't worry; if tofu is not your thing you will be able to wash it down with yesterday's sewage.

"We now consider parts of Earth to be Biohazard level 4," continued Soukup. "Anyone entering from the locations we are calling hot zones without first being confirmed to be clean, will be treated as potentially infected as of now. I will alert you to any changes of protocol, good luck."

"I think I will enjoy my coffee," said Diane, "I may not get to enjoy coffee for a while now."

"They have coffee plants," said Tone.

"Not so many that I can always have coffee," said Diane. "Some idiot decided we needed soybeans instead."

I glanced at an email. "So, it looks like I will be giving a presentation," I said.

"So, you are the one who gets to give the 'how much trouble are we in' report," said Diane. "I don't envy you, good luck."

I began the 'How Much Trouble Are We In' report at 10:00 in the morning, in the station's full auditorium.

"Ok, so here is the first problem," I began. "From what we know there are at least 24 separate species of pathogen from *Hortus* capable of infecting humans. Thus far they have not shown any sign of being stopped, or even being slowed down, by our immune system, our best medicines, or any level of toxin that would not do more harm than good. These *Hortus* pathogens are Beta Strain life. Given the nature of Beta strain we can deduce that it is incredibly tough, and will be very hard to deal with.

"Beta Strain microbes can survive higher temperatures, colder temperatures, more radiation, and higher doses of every antibiotic known to man than Earth life can. Things that are toxic to Earth life, these little microbes take in without a problem. So, anything that we can throw at them will kill Earth life faster than we kill the pathogen, if we even can damage it at all. So conventional treatment will be at best, useless.

"If these pathogens are capable of infecting other animals, or plant and fungi as well as humans, then we have more problems. Not only do we have to make a cure for humans, we may also have to make and distribute one for all plant and all animal life, otherwise we could be looking at total collapse of the ecosystem and food chain, as well as crop blights, and mass infection and death of livestock."

"We have also tested Beta Strain microbes in the lab. In several tests, we allowed Beta Strain and Earth Strain microbes to compete in a controlled environment, and the Beta Strain microbes won more often than not, only beaten sometimes by more complex Earth Microbes. Against simple Earth microbes however, Beta Strain always won. If the more complex and well-developed Beta Strain

Hortus microbes can outcompete complex Earth microbes than we have another problem.

"If any other microbes hitchhiked a ride to Earth with our pathogens, then we could be facing a second disaster, mainly all our Earth microbes being outcompeted and wiped out, which could have untold consequences for life on Earth, especially if symbiotic microbes are wiped out. However, we have no way of knowing if this has happened, but there are still many candidates that don't appear infectious that may still try to outcompete Earth life, or otherwise cause trouble down the road.

"So, even if we can make a cure, we may also have to distribute it to animals and plants as well as humans, then we will have to save any symbiotic microorganism that keep us, plants, and other animals alive in the first place. We also have to do this without doing more harm than the Beta Strain would, which is difficult as it seems to be tougher than Earth life. Lastly, we will have to find a precision tool, as blunt instruments might kill us first.

"In addition, we don't know anything about how any of the pathogens infect, when a person becomes contagious, and what, if any sign, would be the first sign of an infection and being contagious. But we do know that it can get around our immune systems, and target specific organs such as the lungs. So, it seems that our plague running amok on Earth is more than capable of dealing with our bodies. We also believe that the most common Beta Strain pathogen, Pathogen Six, may be transmittable by air, after all, it attacks lungs. If this is the case, then infection could spread at an alarming rate.

"Lastly, as Pathogen Six is able to take on our immune system, we have to assume that any other *Hortus* pathogens could also survive the immune responses of whatever plant or animal life they find to infect on Earth.

"So, in conclusion, it's tougher than anything we have ever dealt with, smart enough to navigate out bodies, may be part of a group able to infect our entire ecosystem, and, worst case scenario, may bring friends to destroy symbiotic microbes, thus eliminating all native life on Earth. We have no potential treatment that would be better than the disease, which is lethal, and even if we did, we may need to apply it on the scale of the entire biosphere."

"Any questions?" I finished.

No one asked anything.

The next presenter, Dr. Jeffery Cabal, got on stage.

"We have limited time, and can't ask the infection for an extension, so the question of the hour is how much time do we have?

"As for the infection, we can't know. Thus far it has had 100% fatality rate, and has killed within a week of the first signs of infection. As for how fast it can spread, we don't know. Until we know its R value, the rate of infection, we can't say how fast it may or may not spread.

"But it will most likely spread at an exponential rate, now it may be small, but given the time span of infection, if it does spread, which we think it will, it will build up speed the longer it goes. Meaning each week, we can't stop it means that it will spread further and faster.

"What we do know is how long we can last on our supplies; this station is built for long term viability, but we estimate that it will begin to fail within a few decades. Our supply of spare parts is limited and there is only so much we can do to build, or recycle, any damaged parts. Other space stations require more constant resupply, and are projected to fail within a few months of total isolation.

"We may need to find a way to help other space stations survive on limited supplies, or a way for them to trade the parts and materials they need to survive. As well, many sites on Earth may require quarantine. Right now, only 1 site is known, but the panic and distress has caused much of the outer region to be abandoned. Some people left before quarantine could be established. If any of them unwittingly took the pathogens with them, they could spread the pathogens far and wide.

"Even if we successfully quarantined the pathogen, which may not be possible, the disruption to transportation and trade would be disastrous. So, if it breaks out, we can, at best, manage a few years of strict quarantine, if people cooperate, while the infection brews.

"We all hope that the infection may be contained near the epicenter; if it is, we can let it burn out inside if and only if we can keep it contained. However, we have also instituted a quarantine and release program. If it works, then many lives that otherwise would have eventually been infected, may be saved. But we would have to be careful to not release any infected individuals. If we can't make it work, I would bet many would try to escape; that could potentially spread the infection further."

Dr. Cabal ended his short presentation, at which point Dr. Foster took the stage via vid screen. She was the only person presenting who was not physically present.

"For the time being I am remaining on Earth to direct the situation from the ground. Quarantine will most likely fail and soon; many people are attempting to leave the site of the infection. If any of them are carriers who do not yet show symptoms, then they could take our pathogen far and wide and destroy any attempt to maintain containment.

"We do not know if any of the pathogens are moving through the ecosystem yet. If they are, or can, then we will likely be unable to contain it even with perfect cooperation from people in the infected zones. For now, we are attempting to keep the public calm, but I don't know how long this can last.

"Our next task will be identifying the rate of the infection. It is possible that these pathogens have no mechanism for spreading in humans, but I would not get your hopes up as we already know it can infect lung tissue and trigger coughing. It may be possible that they can travel through the air, which would drastically worsen the situation.

"In any case there is nothing we can do now that will help people rather than worsen the situation. If all else fails, we will try to wait it out and minimize the suffering of the infected. However, I want everyone to prepare for the worst possible scenario, because if it happens, then we are talking total extinction of life on Earth. Let us all hope it does not come to that. But if it does, you may need to be ready to help lead whatever of the human race is left."

So, our goal was set: somehow prevent an alien microbe from wiping out all life on Earth. No way to stop it, no way to predict its abilities; we were in trouble.

A week later we had learned more about our enemy. Mainly it spread at an R average value of five. R values are used to calculate infection rate. In the case of an R value of two, as an example, patient zero gets two people sick while they are infectious, those two people spread it to two more people each while they are infectious, at an exponential growth rate, spreading faster as it goes on until it runs out of people to infect.

Dr. Foster had been monitoring the situation and gave us the results; the R value was close to five. Each infected person would pass it to an average of five others before death.

"Five…. So, every person infects an average of five others before death?" asked Diane.

"According to this report," I said. "The body is still infectious after death and those handling must be careful not to get infected themselves. Worse, they did blood tests and got a positive result on people who were showing no symptoms. It looks like they might have been infectious at that point as well."

"So," said Diane. "If someone is infected, they could appear healthy, yet unknowingly infect others."

"Yep," I said, "But we need more data, and well, Tone and I are going."

"Where?" asked Diane, "A hot zone?"

"Yep," I said. "Going to the quarantine zone."

"What, today!!!?" asked Diane, her face looking pale.

"Yeah," I said, "Try not to worry too much."

"Yeah but, the hot zone?" Diane still looked shocked.

"We both took the rush-through of how to use Biohazard gear," I said, "We will be fine."

"If you say so," said Diane taking a sip of coffee, "Still, I think I will reserve the right to worry."

Later I reported to the atmospheric shuttle. I, and the rest of the science team going with me, were already wearing our Biohazard suits. We did one last check and inflated the suits above atmospheric pressure to check for leaks, and to ensure that if they were punctured, they would blow air out, rather than suck it in. This was a last-ditch effort to keep us from getting infected from a puncture. Everyone took a minute to leave a potentially final message; I addressed mine to mom, and we were ready to go.

We landed uneventfully, just outside the quarantine zone in Chile. Our goal was to check the surrounding area for any signs of infection. My first glance was not hopeful; my view included a dead bird, and the trees seemed to be turning brown as well, even though summer had just officially begun here. Nevertheless, I started by collecting a soil sample; we got this thing to Earth on a soil sample so maybe it was hiding here as well.

Tone headed into the quarantine zone, I stayed outside to see if the containment was holding.

Looking around, some of the trees were dead, and there were dead animals littered throughout the area. While gathering a soil sample, I spotted a deer lying dead on the ground. One of the other scientists walked over to get a sample from the animal.

I tried to keep going; even insects were lying everywhere. I tried to look for something alive, but found almost nothing, everything I saw was dead or dying.

I looked at the fence. On the other side was the quarantine zone. Every instinct I had said, "This does not bode well."

Much of the outlying town was abandoned. If you looked around you could see some houses that still had their lights on. But even then, it looked like everyone was packing, frantically.

After several hours, which felt like a lifetime, I caught up with Tone on the shuttle.

"How did it go?" I asked.

"It was depressing, it feels like, well, death," said Tone. "Like, there was a pile of bodies outside of the hospital, where they were just piling them up because there was no place to put them... I think they were going to try and burn them."

After a quick decontamination, we sent our samples to the laboratories and went to meet with the scientist analyzing the first group of results. To my surprise I found Diane running one of the labs.

"Hello again," I said.

"Avery! Tone! You're, ok?" she exclaimed.

"Should be," I said. "No suit breaches as far as anyone can tell, nothing other than a perfect mission; everything went smoothly."

"That's a relief," she said. "Also, the first good news I have had all day."

"So, there is bad news?" asked Tone.

"Yeah, well, no containment breached up here yet, so I suppose that is good," said Diane. "But, well, first glances towards break out are not good, the soil was infiltrated with Beta Strain microbes, and our old friend Pathogen Six came up again and again and again."

"Ok, what about the trees?" I asked.

"We may be on the verge of identifying a problem with them as well, something else is infecting them, also Beta Strain." said Diane.

"The patients at the hospital?" asked Tone.

"Almost entirely Pathogen Six, so far."

"So, one less problem to worry about," said Tone, "I mean, no other pathogens in the system."

The look on Diane's face indicated otherwise.

"What is the catch?" I asked.

"You didn't happen to find any dead insects, did you?" asked Diane.

"There were a lot of cockroach corpses, and spider and fly bodies," said Tone. "Although my job was just collecting samples from human patients; I didn't have anything to collect insects with."

"I got samples of dead insects though," I said, "Why?

"Well," began Diane, "The samples of warm-blooded creatures, mammals, birds, large and small, are mostly Pathogen Six. But cold-blooded animals, reptiles and amphibians, have more of Pathogen Three. We think that one is more adapted to the cold-blooded creatures of *Hortus*. So, they thrive in our cold-blooded friends."

"Is there a different one for insects?" I asked.

"Seems to be Pathogen One mostly," said Diane. "Fish Have Pathogen Seven, and four to five different pathogens infect plants."

"Let me guess, even the soil is overrun?" asked Tone.

"How did you know?" asked Diane.

"Besides the fact that these germs got to Earth in a soil sample?"

"Well, yes, we are still running that test, but at first glance not only have we lots of Beta microbes, but Earth ones are rarer," said Diane.

"So, we are facing worst case scenario," I said.

"If the final results for the soil confirm it, then yes," said Diane.

By the next day, we had confirmed the problem in the soil, wiping out Earth microbes as well as everything else. After some more tests on the soil samples, we found that the Beta microbes had effectively eliminated any symbiotic bacteria in the soil.

I had a hypothesis about how they might be infecting trees. So, we began looking at the fungal network. Forests often have symbiotic fungi, trading nutrients and water the trees need for the sugar the fungi need. I suspected that they might be acting as a conduit, with the tree pathogens moving through them that way. I was right, which really ruined my day.

This was getting out of hand, everywhere we looked, we saw problems, these pathogens could navigate as if they owned the place, and nothing on Earth was so unfamiliar to them that they couldn't find a way around it.

"I'm guessing that complex life on *Hortus* must have similar structures to complex life on Earth," said Diane.

"It's like it knows us, but we don't know it. I'm not sure it could be much worse if this was engineered by some mad man," I said.

"You don't think that this was deliberately engineered, do you?" asked Tone.

"If I thought it was possible, I would think that," I said, "But I doubt it, I think we are just unlucky." I thought for a moment "After all you can't win if you are also dead."

"It could just be convergent evolution," said Diane.

"Same solution on two different planets, and microbes that exploit one planet will work on the other?" I asked. "It could be the problem."

"Might be enough to kill us all." said Diane.

Chapter 5

We had focused our efforts on Pathogen Six, as it was responsible for most of the human infection. Our efforts to find something that would kill it, that wouldn't also kill its host, had been fruitless.

Sure bleach, radiation, cyanide, and a variety of other materials and methods would kill it and other Beta Strain life. But it took too much, we had been testing it on rats, and the amount of bleach needed to kill Pathogen Six killed the rats as well. It also killed any Earth microbes on the rat, or in the rats' cage. In fact, after it killed all the rat germs the bleach then turned the results into goop, well before Pathogen Six was even affected at all. Doing this in the infection site was right out of the question, save for a last-ditch desperate attack.

We needed a precision tool, like many antibiotics, that would be lethal to the microbes, but harmless to humans, at least as long as we did not use too much. Of course, Pathogen Six was all but immune to any antibiotics we could throw at it. Again, we killed our rats before we killed their infections. A target-specific poison would probably do the trick, but we had not found one.

I had been studying the biochemistry of the microbes up close, and taking into account what we knew from other encounters of Beta Strain organism, and what we already knew. I was looking for a weakness, some chemical process we could disrupt, and I found nothing new, no crucial process unique to these microbes. I decided to discuss it with Diane over lunch.

"Why, why are these things so tough?" I asked, "It's like they were already exposed to any and every thing that can kill a microbe and adapted to each one."

"We have seen it on 3 different planets thus far," said Diane, "Meaning that it likely traveled on an asteroid billions of years ago. If this goes back far enough, over enough planets, how many things could they have been exposed to over the eons?"

"So, we are billions of years behind schedule?" I asked.

"Maybe?" said Diane taking a sip of coffee, "If they adapted to it, and then saved the genes, they could still be immune."

"But, wouldn't they have lost that adaptation? If a feature doesn't help for long enough random mutation would make it vestigial, useless. There would be no evolutionary pressure to maintain it. So why is it still strong?" I asked.

"If there was a repeat exposure, then maybe. Every so often, revamping the genes could be enough to get them saved, or over the long term, purposed into something that might have a useful byproduct," said Tone.

"Or maybe this is like a water bear," said Diane. "Those microscopic animals are tougher than they need to be. They can survive the vacuum of space, no reason why they should, but they can and do survive it without trouble. Maybe Beta Strain life is like that, needlessly tough."

"Dang," I said, "OK, any good news on your end Diane?"

"Well for now it seems to be mostly within the quarantine area and around it, spreading slowly. We have to be careful but maybe, we can keep it in the small area in Chile," she said. "Also, one person has actually recovered."

"What?" I asked, "When? How?"

"Well, she lived, barely. It's not exactly pretty though."

"What do you mean?"

She showed me the report, and I almost felt sorry for the survivor. She was on oxygen and had several boils on her skin. There was also a mention of her being in a coma. It didn't mention how she had survived, or what had worked.

"There is a whole team trying to figure out why she lived," said Diane. "Thus far they have found nothing."

"What about her antibodies?" I asked.

Diane looked up from her drink. "They are testing that now, but results are not exactly promising. No change as far as they can tell, it's possible that she is just a fluke."

"So, we just have to hope that the infection stays in its cage?" I asked.

Diane sipped her drink, "For now all we can do is quarantine, and hope for the best."

It was time to change the subject. "How is your family holding up?" I asked.

"David is taking care of Olli in our quarters. Lady seems OK so far with it." She took a bite of eggs. "How is Robey?"

"He is fine," I said, "Probably doing better than I am."

Not even a day later, we got a call about what looked like some cases in New York State. I was dispatched with Tone to check them out.

This time the landing was more eventful. The infection was in a small city, Orick, and word had spread of the infection. The areas where the infection had shown up were placed in quarantine. The people knew that there was an infection on the loose, several people had already been admitted to the local hospital. It was winter, meaning the dead looking trees didn't mean much, but the browning conifers set off alarms. It looked like the same set of symptoms we saw in Chile, at a distance.

This was causing distress to the locals; they wanted to leave. They were afraid that they would die if they didn't. Anyone who could leave was packing like there was no tomorrow. Half of the businesses were closed as all their employees and customers had fled. The people inside the quarantine zone were even more restless.

The biggest difference was that PPE, personal protective equipment, had been distributed. But what most people were getting was far less effective than what I had on. Most were lucky to have a face mask.

I saw that they were trapped in a small area, with death itself. Sure, they had set up a secondary quarantine and release area so that they could let healthy people out, but it was too difficult to maintain well for a large number of people. So slowly, a few lucky people might move from the primary quarantine to the secondary, and could then spend a week hoping they were still healthy enough to be fully released. Meanwhile thousands had already died in Chile, and they were now in the same boat.

Even without the threat of death by an unstoppable alien plague, they were faced with soldiers, armed to the teeth and wearing biohazard suits with the combat gear, guarding a hastily built, but tall, and sturdy, fence. It was patrolled constantly to catch anyone who might try to cut their way out. Several holes were forming, although they don't think anyone had escaped, or rather escaped and not gotten shot by one of the guards.

This was taking a toll on the soldiers as well. The last armed conflict of any significance was over fifty years ago. Many people saw the army as a tradition left over from when it was really needed to defend and protect their home nation. Ever since the G.R (Global Republic) took charge over the entire Earth, there was no real enemy to protect against. Armed forces were smaller than ever, and while still considered a very honorable thing by many people around the globe, very few people enlisted. Of those who did, only a small portion stuck through the training to become soldiers, and most soldiers never saw combat. Even then those that did usually were going up against violent extremists, or particularly brutal criminal organizations that were just too much for local police. In other words, the worst of the worst, often with vastly inferior tech. Our soldiers were not usually up against someone defending his nation with as much effort, or ability, as they had. But rather a crazy person for whom there was little doubt that shooting them was doing a favor to humanity.

But now, now they were being asked to keep a bunch of scared, innocent, non-combatants, the very people they signed up to protect, inside a cage so that they could die in there. The last thing any of them ever thought they would be asked to do. It was hardly the uneventful term of enlistment most of them were probably expecting. Modern soldiers rarely see combat, with something that requires strike team emerging maybe once a decade. Most soldiers did ceremonial work or disaster relief. They would not be told to "Expect to be containing civilians in a fenced in area at gun point". It was not out of the question that some of the soldiers then might want to, or have tried to, rescue some of the people in the quarantine zone. We had not caught anyone doing that, but given everything else going on, it was possible.

Then, we showed up. Anyone still thinking this might not be serious probably had their last dash of optimism destroyed when the GHA (Global Health Administration) people showed up in full biohazard gear, meeting up with the soldiers so that we could get inside the quarantine zone safely. Probably sent the message, "Yep, you are going to die."

Lots of people looked up when we got in. I felt like they were judging me, as if I was a monster come to take them to their ultimate fate. Or else leave them here to die.

Some ways in, but fairly far from the main infection, a little kid approached me and said, "Mommy says you are going to save us. You're going to save us, right?"

I couldn't tell the truth; that we had no idea how or if we could save him. "We will do our best to save you, and everyone here," I said.

The kid smiled, walked away, and I could only hope for his sake, and for everyone's that I was right. That we could save these people before it was too late. My brain said it was impossible, that it was too late for anyone inside the quarantine zone. My heart said we had to at least try. Even though I like to think of myself as a rational person, I decided to follow my heart.

Others seemed to regard us with suspicion, eyeing us from a distance. Sometimes I could see little kids running away and hiding, as if we were going to take them away. I couldn't really blame them; we were the people who said that they had to be contained here, in a place full of death. I'd be distrustful too.

As we got closer to the heart of the infection things changed, the area was wider than the one in Chile. Much of the outer zone looked healthy. But its core looked very different. The region outside the quarantine zone was sparse but you could still find people walking about. Near the heart of the infection however, it looked like a ghost town. Most of the people who lived just outside of the quarantine zone had left; those inside stayed close to the outer walls.

We moved towards the center, where the "Hospital" was located. To be fair it was actually a real hospital, but they had moved many of the uninfected patients outside, to slow contagion for those just looking for a checkup or for a broken bone.

We moved towards those who were infected, inside the actual building, to collect blood samples. We started with those who had only recently gotten infected; they showed the same symptoms as in Chile: fevers, sweating, cough, but there was something else. They appeared pale, paler than they should have. I asked one of them if I could collect a sample of blood. The way she moved, the way she talked, sounded almost as if she had already resigned herself to death. She didn't even wince when I pricked her finger. Once I put the sample away, I said "Thank you, we'll fix this, I promise."

"It's too late for me, isn't it?" she said, finally speaking.

"What um…," I started…

"Don't lie to me please. Just tell me. Am I already a dead woman?" she asked.

It took me a few seconds to figure out the words "I… I don't think we can save you specifically, but… we know of one person who survived, so the odds aren't completely at 0."

She looked away and said, "Do what you can, for everyone else."

"You're a very brave woman," I said before walking away, trying not to think of the fact that the "survivor" would likely be crippled for the rest of her life, if the residual effect of the sickness didn't kill her first. I hoped I could be half as brave if my time came.

I moved on through the relatively healthy patients to ones who were more progressed, to someone who reminded me of Elia, not through his face, but well, Elia looked about as bad during his final hours. The man was awake when I walked in. I asked if I could take a blood test. No sooner had I packed up, then he uttered "Thank you," and his EKG flat lined.

"Um nurse!" I shouted and someone in a hazmat suit came running, not one like ours though. This suit was more makeshift, it might provide enough protection to save someone, but it was nowhere near as good as the one I was wearing. And for the nurse, the risks were far greater than mine.

Still the nurse rushed in, saw the EKG, and grabbed the defibrillator. My escort dragged me away, "We have to move on," he said.

After that the patients started blurring together. A little old man, a girl who couldn't be more than 3 years old, a middle-aged man, in the first stages, just sobbing on the floor. One of the patients I was going to see was already dead of an over dose. I never asked whether it was suicide, accidental or an attempt at mercy, but I thought it could be any.

Then it was time to collect samples from the recently deceased. The morgue had over filled, so they were piling the bodies up in a mass grave outside, and there were more soldiers to keep people away. Canisters of something, maybe gasoline, kerosene, ethanol, were scattered around and being poured onto the pile. Some flame throwers were also present, as well as wood, grass, paper, anything that would burn, some of it was already lodged into the body pile. I saw the same man who I had collected samples from a few hours ago, the one who had thanked me, dead in the pile.

I collected more samples from the dead, from what looked like a pregnant woman and a young child. Many of them were still warm, only a few hours' dead. Robots moved around the site, but there were not enough of them, even humans worked here with what protection they got.

One man was walking around without a suit, or any protective gear beyond gloves and a face mask. I had to ask, "Sir" I said, "Why do you not have a biohazard suit."

"Huh," he started, "Oh, I don't need one, I am already infected, just not feeling it yet."

"Shouldn't you be in bed?" I asked.

"He asked to help," said one of the nurses. "Said that there was no harm to it."

"I am already a dead man," he said, "This might be the last day I feel good, and I want to use it for good."

That caught me off guard. I could understand the logic of it. But it was another thing to see the idea in action.

"Good luck," I said before walking away with my guard.

On the walk back I asked my guard, "How are you holding up?"

"Not well," said the guard. "I was talked out of resigning three times so far. How about you?"

"I... we are clinging on, trying to fix this, it's not... you don't see it up there, but coming down here really brings it to scale," I said. "Up there we can read off the tallies, but down here, it feels more real."

"Be honest... Do you have a plan to deal with it?" he asked.

"No, not yet," I said. "We are trying to make one, but, everything we can throw at it... it just shrugs off. Using brute force, we might do as much damage as this pathogen could do."

"Maybe that... could that be worth it?" asked my guard.

"No, we would just be killing these innocent people faster. Nothing we can do will fix this. Right now, it's better to try and contain it, and see if we can find a cure while slowing its spread." As I said this a part of my mind asked, *What if there is no way to save them, what if the best solution is as the solider suggests? Euthanize the infected to save the rest of the world?* In my mind, I knew the situation was not that bad yet, though it might still get worse. Still, no one was ready to do any euthanasia on mass. We were scientists, not killers.

"So, what can you do?" asked the solider as we got to the gate.

"We are hoping to find a precision treatment," I said, "Not brute force but a subtler lock pick. Our next attempt is to maybe engineer a vaccine."

I tried to ignore the challenges, as it required that we first kill or weaken the pathogen enough that it wouldn't kill the person we vaccinated, and even that might not be enough to provide protection. At times, it felt like this thing was damn near invulnerable.

"On behalf of everyone here, I wish you the best of luck," said the soldier.

"Thanks," I responded, "I think we need it."

I then headed over to the shuttle, which was primed and ready for take-off.

Tone had sampled nature this time, or rather he looked at the flora and fauna in a park near the infection zone. He found a lake, apparently.

"There were dead fish everywhere in the lake," he said holding his head in his hands.

"And the trees?" I asked.

"We did some tests, dead too," he said. "How was the inside, with all the people?"

"Horrible," I said. "I think some of the people I got samples from had...given up."

"Wow, this is, sad," he said, "I was... I was hoping that this would be better than the site in Chile."

"But no, it's just as bad here as it was anywhere," I said.

I hoped there were no other sites like this.

Chapter 6

Over the next month, several more sites popped up across the globe. The days of it being just two hot zones, across North and South America, were over. Now every continent except Antarctica, had them; all the space stations and lunar colonies that could, placed themselves in quarantine to avoid Pathogen Six and the microbes that followed in its wake of death.

This time Diane was doing the presentation.

"So, we have lost control of pretty much all of the quarantine zones, riots are frequent, and what control we do have is mostly through people who have resigned themselves to death, or are hoping for a miracle. About half of the infected areas had no known movement to or from them, indicating either that Pathogen Six is moving with animal migrations, the weather, or through unknown human movements."

"Many agricultural areas are showing crop blights, as well as livestock die-offs; food is starting to become an issue in places. Some areas are going into a sort of reverse quarantine but given the ability of the infection to spread outside of quarantines areas through animal migration and wind it's only a matter of time before an infection occurs. Any place trying to seal itself off, aside from a space station or lunar colony, may only be delaying the inevitable at this point.

"Many space stations are also noting issues. Those that remain infection free are planning to trade with each other to keep their goods and services going. But almost all of them require parts manufactured either on Earth, or on larger space stations that require raw materials. The only other source is the lunar colonies, many of which are also reliant on Earth for some of their resource needs. This includes resources that, historically, they have only managed to import from Earth. To make matters worse the number of people leaving Earth fleeing to the stations and colonies has, at best, strained their resources even further, at worst brought Pathogen Six to them.

"Also, the Global Republic Parks Service has noted massive die-offs in many natural parks of both flora and fauna. Currently the damage is mostly contained within the various infection zones, but those zones are getting bigger by the day. Currently the estimated death count is just in the hundreds of thousands, but we estimate more deaths from famine and secondary infection as this goes on.

"The survival rate remains, within a rounding error, at 0%. And so far, those few who do survive have ended up crippled. Introducing antibodies from the survivors hasn't helped anyone else. If we can't stop this soon, then we may not stop it at all. Currently I estimate that if the infection continues at its current pace, within 10 weeks, there may be no human life on Earth.

I was thinking; we needed something in a package that Beta Strain microbes would absorb easily, but not something Earth microbes would absorb. This something then needed to be very destructive, but that would not last outside the host cell. In other words, it needed to be specific to Beta Strain, quick, deadly, and have no lasting side effects. Or at least not be as bad as wiping out all life on Earth.

The answer to kill off all of the infected, or potentially infected, was becoming more appealing. However, the infected count was high enough that we were no longer sure it was possible to pull off. The option once too horrible to consider, now more tempting, was painfully out of reach. I began to wonder if we should have taken that option when we might have had the chance.

I pondered this while making another collection run with Tone and our respective teams. We were both going inside this time. The site was in Agunu, Nigeria, and of course people were panicking there too. Again, the streets were empty up until the quarantine zone, with death seeming to emanate from it. Once inside everyone looked at us as if we were death himself. As if we had abandoned them to die. I could almost fool myself into thinking I was still in the South American or North American site. Or any of the other sites I had visited.

I was in the middle of sampling when I noticed the yelling. Someone had started a riot and they were heading our way. My guard said to me "We have to go," and so we ran to the nearest safe location. With rioters on the loose it was best to keep our heads down.

Some of our escorts broke off to confront the crowd, while the others took us out the back door. Some of the patients looked scared, others seemed ready to go join the crowd. I could hear the guards trying to calm down the crowd outside.

"People please, stay calm, we are trying to help you, they are trying to help you, please give them a chance," said the commander of the guards.

"So, you lock us in here to die, is that your version of 'helping' us?" someone shouted back.

"As long as you are still breathing there is hope, but this is bigger than us, this is a threat to everyone and containing the spread of infection is necessary, however unpleasant it may be," said the Commander. "I understand your fear, but fear gets us nowhere."

"Are you sure, or is that just what your boss wants you to think; that you're helping save all humans when really you're only saving them," said another voice from the crowd. "They're up there in their cozy space station while we suffer and die."

"If they wished to wait it out then why come down here?" asked the guard captain. "Why not simply hide up in orbit? They have chosen to come down here to help save us all. We have not been abandoned."

"Yet they come wearing suits to protect them from us, why can't we get any?" asked a voice from the crowd.

"There are only so many suits, and so many who are sick, you have seen the makeshift ones the nurses use," said the captain. "We are all strained here, even 'up there' as you put it, they can only stay so long. They have to fix this; they will fix this."

"Then why..." a voice in the crowd began before it was cut off by a gun shot.

I don't know who fired that shot, or where they aimed, but suddenly the crowd started yelling, more gunfire, and an explosion. I briefly glanced over to see that a fire had started. Our escort shouted, "Move!" and suddenly we were running.

After we stopped I surveyed the environment while one of the soldiers took charge.

"Everyone check each other's biohazard suits, once we are certain we are all free of any punctures, we will try to assess the situation." I found Tone and I checked his suit; it was fine. Our new leader called her superiors. Eventually she turned back to us.

"We are cut off from the main entrance and exit by the crowd. If we can lay low and move toward the exit, we might be able to get out with a little help. For now, we move toward it, keep your heads low, soldiers, non-lethal force only." The soldier who had taken charge gave us those instructions. Her badge said Lieutenant Zabia Sall.

Once we approached the exit, Sall gave us the next part of the plan.

"The outside forces are going to try a trick with tear gas once we are ready. Hopefully it will disperse the crowd enough for us to get to the exit and get out, but we will have to move fast," she began. "The crowd may only stay dispersed for so long. Our suits will protect us, but the gas will make it difficult to see. I can't risk taking us any closer so once we get the go ahead we will run towards the exit; follow my lead and keep your heads down. Get ready."

After one final check of our suits, with no signs of damage, and once everyone was ready, Sall decided it was time.

"Alright, on my mark everyone," she said, "3...2...1...mark."

And with that we were running, and as fast as we could go in those suits, we approached the exit. Soldiers on the other side had launched tear gas canisters over the fence; the crowd dispersed. But the canisters were launched too early, the gas began to dissipate, and the crowd began to return.

Soldiers on the other side of the fence began firing warning shots, into the air. No one was getting shot or was at risk, but it was still disconcerting to run towards gunfire. I must have tripped because I found myself face down in the dirt. I got back up right away, but far behind everyone else.

The crowd had nearly returned, still I made a break for it, ran towards the exit, more gun fire. I could see them firing at the air, the crowd dispersed just enough and I got through the fence.

"Are you OK?" asked Sall.

"Yes," I said at first, before noticing that the pressure of my suit had dropped, "No, I think my suit has a leak."

Tone did a quick look, "It's on your knee cap" he said before reaching into his tool kit for a repair item, namely duct tape, "It doesn't look too bad, how low was the pressure?"

"1.1 atmospheres," I said, "I tripped on my way over, so maybe that's when the puncture happened?"

"Maybe," said Tone, "You might not be infected."

"I sure as @#$% hope not," I said feeling sweat beading on my head. "Sorry that slipped out."

"Let's get you to your ship," said Sall, "I understand the protocol is to take him into quarantine and hope for the best."

"Yes," said Tone, "We take him up, lock him away, and wait a few days; if there is no sign of infection, he is released a few days later."

Well either that, or one of the tests would come back with a positive for an infection. This had happened to three people thus far. If it happened to me, I'd write my will, say good-bye to my friends and family, and hope for a relatively painless death. Pathogen Six seemed to go with the slow and horrible death route, but maybe I would get a lucky break.

I made my way to the shuttle, feeling for the first time what many of the people in the quarantine zone probably felt; dead. Sure, there was a chance I was fine, that my suit's positive air pressure pushed out anything trying to get in. Or that the second layer was still intact underneath; it wouldn't be until decontamination that we could find out.

Once docked we went through the airlock and I went into my own separate decontamination booth. I cleaned off my suit and once through the showers, took a look at the under layer of my suit. If it was fine, then so was I. Sure I might still have to spend time in observation, but there would be no way that anything got through.

But the under layer was also damaged, and in any case, I had to shower off a second time. I still had a respirator on, just in case. After a third shower, I showed the doctors through the viewing window the damage on the inner layer.

"@*#%," said the doctor, "Ok where was this on your body?"

"My left knee cap," I said.

"Show me," said the doctor, "Show me your knee."

I brought my knee cap up to the glass and pulled back my pant leg.

"OK I don't see any injury," said the doctor, "But we still need to put you in quarantine."

"I know, I know," I said.

"We might as well get to know each other," said the doctor, "I'm Doctor Alex Fry."

"Doctor Avery Hutton," I said back, "Where to from here?"

"Quarantine is down that hall way, your room is the third door," said Dr. Fry.

I went down to the third door as instructed, and entered. It was a one-person room with a bed, I changed out of my work clothes, and into a hospital gown laid out on the bed. After putting my regular clothes in the hopper, I pushed a button to open up the view screen. Dr. Fry was there already.

"OK, good you have changed. We have a robotic setup for interaction. This will mean that no one has to change into biohazard gear to get in and out," said Dr. Fry "First we need a blood sample."

I went to the diagnostic station and placed my finger in the designated position and waited for the prick.

"Ouch," I said as it gathered a small blood sample.

"OK, we also need to check your breath. Pathogen Six seems to be airborne so that is our next test."

A mechanical arm bought out what looked like the nozzle of a Breathalyzer. I took a deep breath, and blew into the machine with all my might. It made a ringing noise, which meant to keep going, it kept ringing for what felt like a minute, by which time I was out of breath. It finally dinged 'done'.

"Ok, we will also need a urine sample," said Dr. Fry.

A machine dispensed a cup. I took it to the restroom to provide them the sample; it took a while and some running water for 'inspiration', but once I had a sample, I put it in the box for urine samples. I washed my hands and then exited the rest room.

"The cup is in the box," I said.

"OK" said Dr. Fry, "That's it for today, I will let you know the results as soon as they are done."

I went to the bed to lie down, hoping against hope that I was alright. I tried to not cry, or at least to not make any noise while doing so. I might still be ok, right, that puncture was why our suits used positive pressure, we noticed and patched it up right away; it should be ok, right.

But it was still a breach of my suit in a hazardous environment, one with a deadly microbe running amok. I could still die, in agony as so many already had, like Elia, and the others on the station. Like the thousands who already went through this on Earth.

Elia was so brave facing death, so calm. So was the man who died in front of me at the North American site. Could I be that calm, or would I panic and try to escape? I couldn't escape, shouldn't escape, I could contaminate the entire station. That could kill everyone on it and destroy one of the last things standing in the way of what might be the deadliest pathogen ever discovered by man.

But I felt like a dead man in here, like this was my tomb, where I had been taken to die. That if I did not escape, I would die. I knew that was not true, that if I escaped I would either die or live with my location not mattering at all... How did Elia, the man who died on me, and so many of the others keep so calm? How did they face death so well? I wish I could be half as calm as they were... I think I understood the people who rioted... #$%$ this sucks.

Chapter 7

So, I was maybe infected with a deadly disease, as were lots of other people; nothing I could do about either, all I could do was hope for the best. Still after seeing that so many people like Elia, like the other scientists, and like many of the sick and dying had remained hopeful, or at least brave in the face of doom, I found myself with a question. How in the name of everything did they do that, because I was absolutely terrified?

How did they feel themselves dying, and force themselves to fight on; how did they push forward knowing that they were going to die? I was (maybe) going to die, and every thought in my head told me I was already in a grave. Just a big one with lots of fancy medical equipment.

Nothing to do now but try to get some sleep. A difficult prospect when I might wake up tomorrow and find out that I was doomed. To be fair, sleep had been a rare occurrence since I got here. It was stressful and scary, and every day brought more bad news. The two most consumed items were sleep aids and coffee, followed by other stimulants. Although the majority of station occupants did not have the nagging feeling that they might be dead by this time next week.

The next morning, I woke up stiff and sore. I had not slept well, even for the standards of Failsafe station. I had multiple nightmares about a moment now only a few hours away. When Dr. Fry would come back with my results, if he had them yet. If he didn't, then well I would have to sit here and worry for a few more hours while waiting for the confirmation of my death. But first breakfast.

A small tray of scrambled eggs was ready for me at 7:00 AM. Dr. Fry came with them, the eggs went through a small air lock for letting things in, and Dr. Fry talked to me through the window.

"No sign of infection yet," he said through the speaker, "Too soon to tell but it is a good sign."

"When will we know for sure?" I asked.

"Previously the first symptoms showed up a few days after exposure," he said, "Blood test results will come back sooner, speaking of which we will need a new battery of tests as soon as you have eaten."

This puzzled me. "Don't doctors usually need tests to be done without food?" I asked in between bites of egg.

"In some cases, yes," said Dr. Fry, "But in this case, it doesn't matter, also we want to measure your appetite. If you are eating, it is a good sign."

I had heard about some people infected with Pathogen Six, or one of its cronies, refusing to eat or drink. So, I guessed the fact that I was ravenous and thirsty was a good thing.

Sure enough, after eating, I was Dr. Fry's pincushion. Another round of blood tests, breathing tests, and urine tests. Then a long questionnaire about any way I felt different, any potential symptoms, even general health questions.

"Alright, I will send these off to the lab; results should be in by dinner," said Fry before leaving.

I spent the rest of my morning trying to relax in quarantine. Easier said than done, so I turned on the news looking for a distraction. Eric Long was there to begin reciting the day's events.

"The GHA has confirmed that another scientist may have been infected with Pathogen Six while visiting Agunu during the riots. The scientist's name and the location of the incident have been withheld. We contacted Dr. Jane Foster to see if she had any input."

"All I can say," said Foster, "is that this individual has only been potentially exposed and we are keeping track of the scientist's health. Out of respect for personal privacy I cannot say more about how, where, or when the incident occurred, or to whom it occurred."

"What can you tell us?" asked Long.

"That we have put said individual in quarantine for the time being, and that release will be allowed if and when we have confirmed that no infection has taken place. If the scientist is fine, then he or she will be asked to return to duty. If not, we will attempt to keep the person as comfortable as possible while in quarantine until death," said Foster.

"This is the third case of a potential infection of a scientist, in two days" said Long, "Why is that?"

This was my first hint that there were others I didn't know there were two others. To be fair I had been busy.

"We believe that it may be a combination of the frightened public, and exhaustion on the team's part," said Foster, "After all that has happened, and is happening, and what is being asked of both the scientists and the general public, it's hard for me to blame either."

"Still, this suggests danger to those trying to solve this problem," said Long.

"We are of course looking into addressing these issues," said Foster, "But there is only so much we can do without worsening the situation and we are on a tight schedule. Some risks have to be accepted. There are also a lot of other things that require our attention, some accidents are bound to happen."

"Some have complained that the scientists have received preferential treatment when possibly infected," said Long, "They're being quarantined to determine right away whether they are infected or not, instead of waiting with the other possibly infected people. With so many dying on Earth, is there any reason, or justification for this?"

"These men and women may be the key to stopping this plague on Earth," said Foster, "Without them there may be no way forward. They may have the knowledge to save the rest of Earth; I'd say that earns a little more investment given the circumstances. Yes, I know to an onlooker it may seem unfair but, well, no one likes it but we decided that it is necessary in this situation."

"I don't wish to be rude," said Long, adjusting his seating, "But shouldn't we focus on fairness for those infected? After all, one could argue it would help keep people calm."

Dr. Foster leaned forward, "I don't wish to be rude either, but the last time you doubted my calls, with the remains of Dr. Turner, it turned out that my concerns were correct. If you had listened to me then, we wouldn't even be in this situation at all. I think you might owe me some understanding."

So, she was not above an "I told you so" after all.

Long remained silent for a quarter minute before saying, "OK, fair point, but it doesn't change the fact that many people are dying right now of this infection…"

"And we are doing everything we can for them," said Dr. Foster with a grimace. "But sometimes that means we have to do something that, on the surface, may seem hard to swallow."

This time, Long remained silent for what felt like a whole minute.

Dr. Foster broke the silence, "Right now, we are not in a position to fight about what is morally right, we have to look at it logically. Is it fair? No, not by any definition. Is it our best chance to save as many people as possible? Yes."

"Thank you," said Long.

As much as I appreciated Long getting his comeuppance, I couldn't help but wish Dr. Foster had broken that out, just a little earlier.

I had visitors for lunch: Diane and David.

I said, "Hey Diane, David. I didn't expect to see you here."

"Well, I heard about what happened," she said, "So I thought I would stop by for lunch. Also brought this gift."

She passed me something through the airlock; it was a get-well card.

I said, "Thanks Diane, tell Tone I said hi."

"I will in a minute," she said, "I volunteered to take your shift on the next landing mission."

David grimaced and Diane seemed fidgety, "It'll be fine" I said, "I only got caught because of a mob."

"I know but... I'm not used to, or trained in Biohazard level 4," said Diane.

"Well... did they set you up with someone to walk you through it?" I asked.

"Tone," she replied, "On account of us already knowing each other. Even if I used to be his boss."

"There you go, it might be weird, but it will be fine," I said, "Even if something goes wrong the suits are designed to push air out if they get punctured."

"But still there is a risk of infection, right?" asked David.

"Well, yes," I said, "But every mission I went on previously went fine without a hitch," I turned to Diane, "Just keep cool and let everyone else guide you through it."

Diane looked down with a frown. I decided to change the subject.

"Could you update me on Earth?" I asked.

"Huh, oh, sure, no problem," said Diane, "So there were three other riots, two of which were related to GHA personnel coming to pick up samples. We believe the other was an attempt to break the quarantine fence."

"Any new outbreaks?" I asked.

"Several dozen, all of which required quarantine zones," said Diane.

"Any good news?"

"No," said David, "Or if there is neither of us knows about it."

"Any bad news?"

"Well," said Diane taking a bite of her sandwich, "If I had time, I could update you myself, but eventually I will need to get back to work. The news channels can catch you up fairly quickly."

"Yeah, I did some watching earlier, they said two other scientists were exposed?" I asked in between sips of my drink.

"Yeah, one was an accident on the station, the other was related to a fall. Even if that guy is not infected, he still has a broken leg," said David.

"Anything else I should be aware of?"

"Not unless you didn't see Dr. Foster's interview with Long," I could see Diane's smirk.

"I saw, and I liked it," I said.

We then ate the rest of our meal in silence.

After Diane left, and with nothing else to do other than stew, I turned the TV on and went back to the news.

The headline "THE END OF DAYS" really caught my attention.

Eric Long was there with the story.

"It's been a month since the accidental release of Pathogen Six, and many other so-called Beta Strain microbes, onto the planet Earth. Scientists say it has infected hundreds of thousands of people. At its current rate, it is estimated that by the end of the week, there may be over a million infected with Pathogen Six. Scientists from the UNHO say that any attempt to stop the infection with conventional methods would do more harm than good, and that they are not sure anything can be done to stop it at this point."

Another scientist, Dr. Edvard Verner spoke.

"Beta Strain life is incredibly durable, able to withstand and function in conditions that would be lethal to almost all Earth life. In addition to the potential damage, we could cause trying to fix it, even a level of any radiation, or bacterial killing agent that would even have an effect, would take far too long to prepare and set up for dispersal. Even if we decided that we could not risk helping those currently infected."

"So, what can we do, Doctor Verner?" asked Long.

"All we can try is to find some sort of secondary agent," said Verner. "If we can find something to fight it, something that can be launched without destroying all life on Earth, or even prepared in the remaining time, then we have a shot at survival."

"Is there no other way to survive?" asked Long.

"Maybe, but it is a stretch at best," said Verner. "If we can make several sizable shelters that could be self-sustaining for several years, and completely sealed from the outside world, and get a healthy population in there, we could allow a small number of people to survive the outbreak."

"Is that possible?" asked Long.

"Well... maybe" said Verner, "If it works, we could save some people, but it would require enormous effort and resources to pull off. I would not put it as my first option. Currently the best thing anyone can do is try and stay calm. I know it sounds impossible to do in this situation, but we might be able to pull something off. Keep surviving; I promise you we will fight to the last breath."

At this point I decided that I needed to distract myself. Listening to the news was just going to drive me nuts. Doing nothing was driving me nuts... actually this was the first day off I had had in a month... Ok maybe not a vacation... but it's something. And they say that you need to take an occasional break and then come back with a different perspective.

That sounded like a plan: take time to think, maybe have a brilliant idea in this little room. So, I watched some old movie, then another after that... then I did some exercise and had a nice long shower.

Feeling refreshed, I grabbed some paper and started writing down all the things I could think of that killed bacteria on Earth. Then I crossed out all the ones Pathogen Six seemed to be immune to.

Most people, after crossing out antibiotics, DNA damaging agents, anything that is impossible or impractical to pull off with what limited resources we had left, were left supporting the 'hide as many people as we can in some sort of environmental chamber' strategy. It had become a popular strategy, at least in private. I came across something insane; maybe we could use a virus against the infection. No one had tried it yet though, as far as I knew anyway, I circled it as an option to counter the infection.

Why hadn't we tried that? Because there was no Beta Strain virus, that we knew of at least. So, nothing we could make more virulent. That itself was odd, as the other two strains of life we knew of, Earth life and Gamma life; each had a treasure trove of viruses. Nothing in Beta Strain though, we had found nothing virus like.

Releasing another Beta Strain microbe to kill Pathogen Six sounded like doing deliberately what we had earlier done accidentally. Even if it made the situation any better, it seemed unlikely that this would be any better than what we already had available to throw at them, which even in the best-case scenario could leave us only slowing the inevitable.

Although, thinking more about viruses, if Beta Strain did not have viruses, then it would mean that it was something it was not used to seeing. Something new, that it might not have a defense against. Viruses are also usually target specific, so if we found one for our microbes it could probably take care of things.

Problem: Beta Strain life used an entirely different genetic code, first using Uracil instead of Thymine for its equivalent to DNA. The other problem was that the codons meant a completely different thing. It was a different language with some of the same letters but in all different orders. An Earth cell could not read Beta DNA and vice versa. We would have to find a way to translate Beta Strain DNA.

Well, we knew what the base codons meant, what amino acid they coded for, and the result of any given strand. That was discovered a while ago. Maybe that could be used as a cypher. If we could take the DNA of an existing virus, translate its codons to Beta Strain DNA, then we could have a Beta Strain specific virus of doom.

OK, so we would need to make the virus, which we didn't know how to do.

Possible solution: we knew that viruses worked by hijacking healthy cells, inserting their DNA, and forcing the cell to make copies of the virus. If we could duplicate this process, then we would have a virus.

Another big problem was that it was crazy; no one in their right mind would ever unleash an alien virus on Earth. If it figured out other hosts then we would not save the Earth but simply put the final nail in its coffin. This sort of thing is a huge risk.

OK, so unleashing a virus was too risky, but maybe I could use this line of thought to create something that would work. In fact, this idea could still have something worth considering.

Dr. Fry saw the collection of papers on the desk when he came to check up on me and said, "You really should not be working today."

"Sorry," I said, "I just felt like I should be doing something; is there anything I can do from here?"

"Honestly not much, and you shouldn't," he said, "If you have an idea save it for tomorrow."

"Why tomorrow?"

"Because by tomorrow evening, we will know if you will make it. Until then try not to stress."

"I suppose now is a bad time to mention that I spend a lot of time thinking?"

"Yes," said Dr. Fry, "But still save it. If we find out you are infected, you can tell me, if you are fine, you can try it out in your lab."

The next day was agonizingly long, but Tone visited and that helped. He was wearing his one, plain T-shirt.

"The doctor said that I should not be working but I couldn't help myself," I said.

"You didn't do too much did you?" asked Tone.

"Mostly I just got ideas that I wanted to write down," I said.

"Like what?" questioned Tone, taking a bite out of a chocolate bar.

"Mass gene therapy for Pathogen Six," I said.

"Sounds…. ambitious," said Tone.

"I know, but... maybe we could use a retrovirus, then use that to insert a gene that kills it?"

"On that scale? That is a bit much, and if any part of the population didn't work then it's just slowing it down, not killing it."

"Ah, right." I said, "Scratch that idea then."

"Although," said Tone, "This might still help."

"How?" I asked, suddenly very confused.

"We might be able to damage it enough to make a vaccine, some sort of small group that we can control enough to safely use as a vaccine, or to kill the pathogens, and use that to spread immunity."

"Oh, yeah, that could work," I said.

"OK, I will go tell Diane; when you get out, we'll get started," said Tone.

"If I get out," I said.

Later that day the 'if' was removed.

"Good news," said Dr. Fry, "You're fine."

"When do I get released then?" I asked.

"Right now," said the Doctor, and then the door to the outside, separate from the one I came in, opened up. I walked out thinking "OK, I need to tell everyone I am fine." But I was interrupted by Diane, Tone, and David who had come to visit.

"This is the first genuinely good news I have had in a while," said Diane, "And I feel that we need to celebrate. Turns out this place has a bar, I got someone to watch Olli we're going."

"OK, but I don't drink," I said.

"First time for everything." Said Diane

That celebration may have turned me off from drinking forever. No, I didn't drink, but I did get vomited on by Tone, who drank way too much.

The next morning, I looked over our plan. Mainly I tried to figure out what was wrong with it. If it worked, then why hadn't anyone else proposed it? We were looking for a plan; any idea would be good, so why hadn't someone stepped up to say, "Let's try weakening it to make a vaccine?"

Or maybe I was overthinking it. I was simply the first to come up with a virus and propose it. As Dr. Foster said, it was better to at least look into the solution, rather than assume it had been done. I then looked it up and it turned out, no one had tried this idea.

But it was a huge risk. If we got it wrong, and it jumped species somehow, it could make everything worse. But maybe...

The virus could be kept in containment. It could then be used to kill a small number of Beta Strain microbes. Use the remains of the microbes as the basis for a vaccine. And then mass inoculations.

Specific to our target? Check.

Would it kill Pathogen Six? No, but would it make people immune? Maybe.

Easy to do? We already used gene therapy for humans, and sometimes even symbiotic bacteria, mostly to treat diseases. But the facilities existed.

Chance of accidentally making things worse? Not too likely, this was a vaccine, old tech, we knew how to make this work.

Would it stop the other pathogens and Beta microbes in the environment? Probably not, but it got us time.

So, what did I need to make it happen?

A gene that would harm or hinder Pathogen Six, perhaps something like Apoptosis. Controlled cell death.

In humans, this was caused when a cell was infected or otherwise dangerous to the human body. It would destroy itself in order to save the rest of the body. Pathogen Six was single celled, so it had no need for that, but we could hopefully insert the genes for it inside Pathogen Six with some sort of activation mechanism.

So, I had a plan, one that was not completely insane; we needed to do it.

Chapter 8

There was more bad news in the morning; a number of lunar colonies and space stations were reporting cases that looked like Pathogen Six. Some of these sites were mostly self-sufficient, but even then, each colony or station required some resources to come in or go out, or required parts and materials that they could not make themselves. So, most were not in solid quarantine. Some of the larger ones, like Pehelan, had isolated themselves, but with stagnating economies and slowly running out of replacement parts, they could not keep it up forever. We needed to find a solution.

Previously we had tried to keep things going by identifying safe areas, and having them do the trade. This allowed them to keep the economy going, and for stations that needed supplies from Earth to get them, with little risks. While we could stop most human movement it was expensive and caused its own issues. It helped but, we couldn't handle animal migrations and wind patterns. This not only kept Pathogen Six spreading despite our best efforts, it also meant that space stations were occasionally succumbing to Pathogen Six. Diane, Tone, and I were looking at the projections.

I was worried so I called Mom. To my relief she answered, and looked healthy.

"Hi Mom, how is Earth?" I asked.

"OK for now," said Mom, "But there is a quarantine zone nearby."

And now I was worried again, "OK, how close?"

"Oh, 15 miles away," Mom said, "They are offering people nearby a chance to move."

"That's… good?" I said, "You going to take them up on that offer?"

"No," said Mom, "They need help, so I offered, and they accepted."

"Oh, so what are you going to be doing?" I asked.

"I am going in as a nurse," she said, "They are fitting me for a biohazard suit tomorrow."

Somehow everything felt more real when it was happening to a family member. I knew that they needed help. But I was also worried for my mom.   "I will be fine Avery," said Mom.

"I know, just... be careful," I said.

"I will be, see you around," she said before we hung up.

The next day at breakfast, Tone shared some family concerns over breakfast.

"My parents were caught in a quarantine zone," he said.

"Wow, I hope they are ok," I replied.

It was silent for several minutes, eventually Diane spoke up.

"According to these results, there are a million infected right now. The R value of 5 is holding, so another 5 million infected next week," said Diane. "Perhaps several hundred million in a few weeks. So, if this keeps up, in a month or two, Earth is toast."

"Alright," said Tone, "Let's hope that your gene therapy works, for everyone still down there."

As bad as things were, they could still get worse, a lot worse. Although questions like that were becoming less frequent, and there were more and more suggestions of, "let's seal off the infected areas, and destroy everyone and everything in it". When this started, it seemed like overkill, now we knew that it was not enough. There was no way we could pull that off at this point. The only thing we could accomplish with these plans was giving hundreds of thousands of suffering people a quick death.

Our first task was to see if we could translate Earth DNA to Beta DNA. Like our DNA, it used 3 base pairs to create one codon. We knew what each codon coded for, what amino acid, and Beta life used the same ones.

We decided to start easy. We already knew how to sequence Beta life, and our DNA generation worked well enough with Beta DNA. So, all we needed was a good virus. Pathogen Six was very similar to Archaea, so we started with a simple virus that normally infected Archaea.

We got its DNA sequence off the computer, and translated it. Now for the hard part; we didn't know what key they would need to use in order to get into Pathogen Six, but we knew which section of code did that. So, we modified the code, at random, for hundreds of tests, with small samples of Pathogen Six as the test subject.

This was a test run. We needed to know if, first, it was possible to create a virus in Pathogen Six, or if the defenses were too great. And second, if we could make a virus effective against Pathogen Six. No, we didn't want to release a live virus on Earth with no way to control it. We just wanted to deliver a genetic package.

Normally viruses worked by hijacking a cell and forcing it to produce more of the virus instead of performing its normal functions. The new viruses would build up until the cell exploded and died, releasing the virus. We didn't need this to happen for our vaccine to work.

But we did need to know if, or how, we could get inside. Because then we could use that sequence to allow a virus carrying a modified package to use the same key. After that, if we could find the right package, we could release our inactive virus on the world safely. They could still infect Beta cells, but all they could do is deliver the modifications we needed. There would be no second generation, and thus no chance that the virus could learn how to infect cells native to Earth.

We still needed to plan phase 2, mainly what kind of package we wanted to deliver, or even if it worked at all.

"So," said Tone, "How do we want to test to see if this works at all, bioluminescence?"

"Sounds good to me," said Diane.

"Alright let's do it." I said in agreement.

We were still taking baby steps, in this case trying something relatively easy. We manufactured our retrovirus with a small packet of DNA that would make Pathogen Six bioluminescent. Then we inserted it into our Petri dishes, and also set up a control group, and let it cook over night.

The next morning our experiment had shown a result. One of our Pathogen Six samples was glowing.

"It looks like it worked." I said feeling excited.

"Alright, now let's wait for the data," said Diane, "Make sure it is significant."

The final result was that our gene therapy was very successful with 99% effectiveness. So, we had that going for us; if we could get the microbes to die then we had a chance of getting this to work to stop the spread of the infection.

"So, what should we do?" asked Tone, "to Pathogen Six, I mean, for vaccines?"

"I was thinking Apoptosis," I said, "That would leave lots of dead cell bits lying around."

However, here it didn't work. The Beta strain cells weren't designed to die, after all controlled cell death is used to stop cancer or viruses in larger organisms. Pathogen Six seemingly didn't need that, so they resisted the effort and didn't die. In the few cases where the process did work, it worked too well. It killed the cells and left a lot of toxic materials behind, and often destroyed anything that could be used for a vaccine.

"So, back at square one," I said.

"Not really," said Diane, "More like square two."

"Huh?" I asked.

"We know we have a method of gene insertion; we just need to modify the correct genes to make it weaker," she said.

"So," said Tone. "If we knew how to slow its reproductive rate, then we could still make a weaker version of Pathogen Six, then we use that as our vaccine, granted, much more dangerous, but still, it could work. Then all we would have to do is disperse it, and find a way to catch the other pathogens, such as ways to distribute vaccines to plants and animals that are causing problems."

"Just one problem with that," I said, "We have no idea what Pathogen Six's growth genes are."

"Wait," said Diane, "We know what other Beta life growth genes look like from previous encounters; maybe Pathogen Six has similar ones."

So, we moved on, looking at the Pathogen Six genome for a similar gene, and finally found it.

"There we go," I said, "The gene for cell birth."

We gave it a new gene therapy, hopefully removing the ability of the cells to divide. After making another batch of viruses and testing it out on our stock. Next morning, we had good news.

"Here is the control," said Tone, holding up the image of a Petri dish full of little blotches. "And here is the experiment group," he said holding up another image of what looked like a clean plate. "It's significant. P value of less than 0.05; we got it."

"Nice," I said but I had a burning question, "How did you get here before me, and already have this analyzed?"

"Huh?" said Tone.

"I was going to get breakfast when I saw you and some assistants were here. Why already?" I asked, noting that he was wearing the same "nicest F****** shirt" he had on yesterday.

"Wait, is it morning?" said one of the assistants, "When did that happen?"

"Not long ago," I said. "Its 7:30 station time."

The look on Tone's face was priceless.

"What's going on?" said Diane with a yawn walking around the corner.

"Uhhhh, we might have lost track of time, the assistants and I, and accidentally pulled an all-nighter," said Tone.

"He got the assistant to do it too." I said shaking my head "Again."

Diane stared at Tone for a solid minute, then she stared at me, I shrugged.

"Go get some sleep," I said "Diane and I can continue this once we get her some coffee."

One breakfast later, and after getting coffee into Diane, we started our next move.

"OK," said Diane, "We have the way to weaken Pathogen Six beyond measure, let's see if our rats take the vaccine."

It had taken two weeks for us to get this far and for the antibodies to build up, during which hundreds of little infection zones appeared, dotted. across the globe. Not all were Pathogen Six, but all were deadly.

Now we began the real test; we exposed our rats to the real thing. The infection still took a week to run its entire course in the rats. During this time, much of Australia fell into protest. Food riots became ever more common, and several quarantine zones were overrun.

I kept hoping that this would be the one, that it would work, but things started badly. The rats displayed many of the early symptoms within a few days and the infection developed as it always had, in lockstep with the control.

"It's too soon to say," said Diane. "Even a small survival rate is an improvement. There is still time for them to get better."

But the rats got worse. About a week after infection, I did the rounds and noticed that we had a dead rat.

"Rats," I said aloud, "Diane, Tone, we have a dead one."

"We do?" asked Diane.

"Yeah, and I know it's too soon to say, but this is not a good sign, is it?"

"Not really, let's keep hoping."

Within a few days, all the rats had died. Evidently Pathogen Six was too tough for even a prepared immune system to handle.

"OK," said Diane, "now what"?

"We still have the possibility of gene therapy." I said "It's a long shot, though."

"Maybe we should drop it, and work on a different project?" said Tone.

He had a point. We had been spending a lot of time on this project, and there were always more ideas, each clamoring for attention. If this one was a no show, we needed to drop it and move on.

"OK then, what's the next idea?" I asked.

Silence filled the room. Almost everything that could be tried had already been tried. Everyone was then told what didn't work, which was disappointing, but it meant that everyone was working in parallel on their own project. Eventually Diane had an idea.

"The protein we made, the one that halted reproduction, let's try finding a way to get it inside the Beta cells, and maybe that will shut them all down."

OK, that was a new one. So, we tried taking the proteins that were created by the genes that we used to halt reproduction and released them en masse in a gene therapy. We tried it on our rats but... well we made as much as we could, but after another week it evidently was not enough.

"Rats," said Tone, "Another dead end."

"First glance says we are going at the same pace as the control," said Diane, "We will know for sure soon, but... we may need a new plan."

After running the numbers, we decided we really did need a new plan.

"OK," I said, "It looks like that did zilch, what is our next move?"

Finally, I came up with an answer, "New package?" I asked, "We can let the retrovirus carry something else."

"Like what?" asked Tone.

Just then an announcement came over the intercom from Dr. Ivan Soukup, the manager of the station.

"I have bad news." he said, ignoring the fact that almost all news was bad news now. "Dr. Jane Foster has caught Pathogen Six."

That was really bad news; she was leading the response on Earth, advocating calm, promising that it could be solved. Her infection did not bode well.

"She has transferred primary responsibility to me, and has also instructed me to assume that there is no way to stop it with conventional treatments. In light of this and the growing number of infected on Earth, now numbering into the hundreds of millions, we are no longer limiting our options to save Earth. As of now, we may consider plans that include isolating any remaining space stations and lunar settlements, and or plans that will destroy all life on Earth, if it takes all the alien microbes with it."

Well, OK, no longer relegated to the realm of sanity and helping people.

"If you have any idea that could help save any portion of the human race, in any way, take it to its absolute limit and test it," said Soukup, "We are no longer going to accept 'this could make things worse' as a reason to disregard a plan. We can't afford to worry about ethics. If you need anything to make a project work, ask me, let other people handle field work, give me something, anything. Good luck."

"Well OK, let's think crazy," I said.

What could we do that could absolutely wipe out life on Earth, and take Pathogen Six with it? Is that crazy? Actually, it might be the only way.

"I have not been down there since my scare," I said, "How bad is it?"

"Very," said Diane. "I was in the Salt Lake quarantine zone recently. And, well, that zone covers the entire city, and almost everyone in it."

"How did that happen?" I asked.

"Apparently, it broke out in multiple places," said Tone. "And, it was one of the isolated reverse quarantine areas so, sort of cramped."

142

"So even the places on Earth that have tried to make themselves infection-proof are now starting to see infections?" I asked.

"Looks like it," said Tone.

I looked at a wall, on it was a map of Earth very decorative. There were a lot of people there, my mother, most of my friends, acquaintances I had known briefly and many more people I didn't know. I was worried and I sat there for a while. Diane and Tone were also silent.

After what felt like an age, my mind started racing. From the basic idea of, "It can't get any worse." I came up with a plan, one that would terrify most people, for a good reason.

"Do we still have that virus?" I asked.

Chapter 9

"If we are assuming that it can't get worse, then why not..." I had trouble saying it, "Why not just release a retooled virus that could infect all the cells, and just kill them?"

Diane and Tone took a minute to just stare at me as if I had grown three heads. Diane said, "You know that could become a problem if the virus learns how to infect Earth cells. I mean previously we were using dead viruses; they could not reproduce. But this one... we could probably manage the risk but if we failed... out of the frying pan into the fire.

"I know it is crazy...", I said.

"You're suggesting a cane toad solution," said Diane.

She was referring to the fact that Australia had once had a problem with sugar beetles in their crops. So, they introduced the cane toad to eat the beetles. But the toads instead tried to eat everything else, and since the toads were poisonous, anything that might try to eat them died. The toads didn't solve the beetle problem, and in fact made everything worse, because the Australians did not realize the consequences of what they were setting up.

In this case if even one of our viruses managed to jump ship to native Earth microbes, then we would have a problem, namely a new live virus running around on a world already in the midst of a plague.

"You know that the whole 'we could do more harm than good' argument was just banned.", I said.

"I know I know," Diane pinched her brow. "But… it sorts of feels like we are trying to fight a forest fire with another forest fire."

There were a few seconds of silence.

"Are we talking 'Fight Fire with Fire' style plan, or a 'Controlled Burn Scenario'?" asked Tone.

"Either works," I said.

Diane looked up for a while before eventually saying, "If this works, and I am not on board with the plan yet, but if we do it, it would be poetic justice in the extreme. Kill a plague with a plague."

"But you still think it is crazy?" asked Tone.

"Well yeah," said Diane.

"Hey. Maybe, we need crazy? This plan is so crazy it might just work."

"Fine, let's do this,"

Having convinced everyone else that this was a good idea, even if it felt like I was invoking insanity, we began planning.

"So instead of the test virus, let's get something more... virulent," said Diane.

"Wait..., why?" I asked.

"Two reasons," said Diane, "First, if this works, it will be because it goes crazy and infects all of our problem pathogens, and second, if things are that bad, we need the very best we can get."

We spent a few hours in discussion before making our selection; a simple, but adaptable DNA virus that had no bells or whistles, just infectiveness. We translated its genome into Beta DNA, and infected a few tests cells. Then came a question.

"So, do we go for broke, test it on all fronts?" asked Tone.

It seemed logical, get as many in one scoop as possible.

"I should think so," I said.

Diane didn't say anything but simply walked over to the containers full of the other major Beta microbes infecting Earth. This was it; we had gone all in on our solution. So, I grabbed some Earth microbes to test as well.

"Just in case it is perfectly picky," I said.

"Sounds good," said Diane.

We exposed our Petri dishes in the experiment group to the virus, and the next day there was good news.

"All the Beta Petri dishes in the experiment group have nothing," said Tone, "It's all dead."

"What about our Earth microbes?" I asked

Tone handed me the data. I looked at the data, and it was exactly what we had wanted initially. The Earth microbes were fine, but the Beta Strain, gone. The control was normal so we had a good first step.

"So, are we going to keep testing this?" I asked, "Or just release it as is?"

There was a long pause before I decided on an answer, "Let's talk to Soukup, let him decide."

I called his number.

"Dr. Ivan Soukup speaking."

"Hello, this is Dr. Avery Hutton, we may have something that could work."

"Where are you? What lab?" asked Soukup.

"114," I said.

"I am on my way," he said.

When he arrived only a few minutes had passed; he looked sweaty.

"Did you run here?" asked Diane.

"Yes. Now start describing your result," said Soukup.

"Why did you run?" I asked.

"Not enough time, no ideas, now you have something?" said Soukup.

I decided to step up. "We created a virus that can infect Beta Strain microbes, we tested it on Pathogen Six and the others, as well as some Earth microbes, and it worked. Not only that, but the Earth microbes were fine."

Soukup smiled, "OK then start an experiment with some rats, and keep me apprised, if you need anything else let me know." he said before running off.

The next day the experiment began. The rats were pre-infected, some several days in; our job was to release our virus and go nuts. We set up the quarantined experiment and unleashed the virus on the control group.

As the week went by our hope soared. Sure, all the rats looked sick. But some in the experiment group looked much better. Many were still at an early stage; the infection was progressing slower. The next bit of news was when we did a blood test. Our virus was doing fine, but Pathogen Six was not.

"It really does have no defense against a virus," I said, "We finally found a weakness."

The good news continued, some of the experimental rats started to get healthier. Most still eventually died, but they took longer. When we ran the rat blood through testing, it took several hours, but at the end we had our data. Pathogen Six was gone from our experiment group, most of our rats even survived to see the end of it.

"It looks good," I said.

"I'm feeling good," said Diane.

Tone plugged the numbers into the machine, and it spit out a fantastic P value.

"It's good," said Tone, "We have statistical significance."

Our streak of luck continued. We tested the cages the rats were kept in; Pathogen Six was not there. The only thing that was there were cocoons of our little virus.

"I think we have something good," said Tone. "I'll call Soukup tell him the good news."

Before he could do that, an alarm went off and suddenly the whole station was in an uproar before we had time to celebrate.

"We have a code 12," said a voice over the intercom.

Code 12 meant that there was some sort of containment failure. Our biohazard suits were self-contained, so we were safe even if the air system was compromised, but everyone else was in trouble.

For now, we stayed in the lab, waiting for something, anything, to be announced. Someone called us from outside the lab; a woman wearing a makeshift biohazard suit.

"How long have you been wearing those suits," she asked.

"Since we went inside this lab, three hours ago," said Diane.

"Okay just checking the logs, stay there for now. Are your suits, okay?"

We did a quick once over. "We're all sealed," said Diane.

"Okay stand by for a minute."

We waited for a few of the longest minutes of our lives while she talked with her superiors over the walkie-talkie.

"Three people in a lab, full gear," she said.

"Okay, Tiffany," said her boss. "Keep them in their suits and send them to section seven."

Section seven was the part of the station that was completely isolated, and mostly unused. Its only purpose was as a safe location for anyone who was not infected, should a breach of containment occur. Sure, there was always a skeleton crew there, but other than that it was empty.

"Okay come on out, keep the suits on, just a quick decontamination of the outer layers," said Tiffany.

We did as she asked and came out wearing the full biohazard gear. She walked us down the corridor to section seven. Another man in a biohazard suit met us there.

"Sign in here," he said, handing us a clipboard with a little piece of paper on it.

It was titled 'Section Seven Entry Form' with a small paragraph that stated: *"In the event of total breach of containment, any people who may not be infected are to report to section seven of the GHA Failsafe station. From this location, you are to assume everyone outside of this location is infected with a level 4 pathogen. Your task is to, first, if possible, help them in any way that you can, second, attempt to contain the incident to this station, third, try to salvage any experiments or data that you can. Your signature will imply agreement with these three goals."*

I signed on the line, and was allowed inside. The good news was that this breach had happened at a time when a lot of people were working on planet side, or in labs. This meant that they were in their biohazard suits. But the bad news was that this only applied to the station's scientists, and some of the military backup we had working with us.

The chefs, janitors, maintenance teams, and most of the non-research staff were considered infected. As were everyone's families and plus ones, many of whom had taken on odd jobs and chores around the station. This meant that the people who could keep the station in working order were all potentially compromised.

Also, there was a line for decontamination and showers, and we had to keep the suits on until then. It was a long wait and it was exhausting, but finally we went through a proper decontamination.

Then we learned about what had happened. Dr. Soukup addressed us via intercom.

"There was a breach in bio lab seven," said Soukup, "One of the biohazard filters was damaged, the air flow was sealed off. Later attempts to repair it inadvertently damaged the second layer of filters. The station has been sealed into sections. Those most likely to be exposed are in sections four and five. All other sections may be safe from infection for the moment, but our hopes are not high.

"All the away teams have been informed and will report to section seven upon the completion of their missions. The rest of us are counting on you. If you can't save us, at least keep trying to save the world. Good luck."

Diane looked worried, and she was the one who had family here...

"Where are Olli and David?" I asked.

"Section one," she said.

"Then they should be fine," I said.

"Yes, but what if they aren't?" said Diane, "What if?"

"They are fine," said Tone, "So long as we keep Pathogen Six from spreading too far."

Diane huffed "Easy for you two to say, it's not your husband and child."

Regardless we had a problem. If we couldn't fix this, anyone who was in sections four and five could die. Most of those people who were infected were probably scientists who were working outside of their suits. Not to mention that if it had gotten into the main population, we could lose all of the people who ran the station, which I didn't know the first thing about doing. In any case we could easily lose lots of people, the people who often made our experiments possible. We not only had a moral obligation to help, but also a strategic one.

So, what could we do, but try proposing our virus solution to Dr. Soukup. I wrote a report on what we had and contacted him.

"What do you got?" he asked.

"We might have something, a potential treatment" I said.

"Send me the data."

After a half hour Soukup called me again.

"Let's try this on the station as soon as you can. This is the best answer I have ever gotten and we need something now. If you need anything I will provide it. I am directing all available personal and resources to be at your disposal, good luck."

Chapter 10

So, we had our goal, to release a virus on an unsuspecting station. Ok, maybe we should plan this out so that if it crashes and burns, it won't be because we failed to think our plan through to the end. So, I spoke with Diane and Tone.

"Do we want this to be a test, or just try to save everyone and hope for the best?" I asked.

"I think we are in a position to throw caution to the wind here," said Diane, "But I also have a question."

"What?" I asked.

"Do we use it as is or do we try to increase its potency?" said Diane.

I thought about it.

"If we mess with it, we might make it less potent, testing would take time we may not have," I said.

"But most of our rats died," said Diane.

"They were pre-exposed to Pathogen Six," said Tone, "But by the time we're ready to go everyone may as well be. Still if we spend time trying to fix it, it might be too late when we are ready. I vote we go as is."

"So, do I," I said.

Diane thought for a moment, "Let's inform Dr. Soukup and get started," she said.

We let Dr. Soukup know what our plan was. The Ethics Board had questions, but admitted that doing nothing was worse. Dr. Soukup had pre-overruled them anyway; we were working before they even had a chance to talk to us. In retrospect that was worrying in many ways.

A lab was turned over to our control and we started cooking up viruses. But there was one stipulation, the Ethics Board wanted to give everyone a choice, either be exposed to our virus, or not. This was the one decision they could make and enforce. Ok fair enough, they had a point, but that choice presented a new challenge. We had to make separate groups for the people who said yes and those who said no. It also meant we had to convince people that our plan was a good idea.

"So, should we do direct or indirect exposure?" asked Tone.

"How do you mean?" I asked.

"I mean, inject the virus directly into people's blood streams," said Tone.

I looked at Diane, who simply seemed puzzled.

"We could ask people in the permission form what they would like," I said, "Just, 'the 'virus through the air' or 'injected directly'."

"I would appreciate that choice in their position," said Diane.

"And it gives me another argument," I said, "You don't have to do crazy unless you want to."

"Then, wouldn't most people just choose indirect exposure?" asked Tone.

"Anyone who thought they were infected might not," I said.

I worked that into my little speech, emphasizing choice.

"How are we going to separate people?" asked Diane.

"Let's see," said Tone, "Those who want direct exposure could then help provide indirect exposure to others, but anyone who wanted to opt out, could be at risk of accidental exposure from either of the directly or indirectly exposed," He paused, "We will have to physically separate the opt-outers."

"We should also have a way to change groups," I said, "You can only get more extreme from each level. You can't be un-exposed and once you are exposed…"

"There is no going to the un-exposed group," said Diane, "But if you knew you were infected, stepping it up might make sense."

"Or we could move people who no longer want to be exposed into their own group," said Tone, "Although this does mean another group to keep track of."

"Actually, that makes sense," said Diane, "Someone probably will change their mind and will need a place to be."

"Ok" I said, "We have enough of a plan for me to make an argument."

We began working out the fine details; eventually we set everything up.

I went to prepare my speech. I needed to inform everyone of what they were getting into, and why.

"So, we have a plan," I said over the intercom, "but I know some of you are not going to like it. My colleagues and I have managed to create a virus that, thus far, seems to only attack Beta Strain microbes, including Pathogen Six. But we have not tested it on humans at this time.

"This is not an experiment, this is an offer of a treatment, one that is untested, but we will not hold it back because we need a control group, we will do proper experiments some other time. For now, we are trying to save as many people as possible. So, you will get what you ask for, nothing more nothing less. There will be no placebos."

"We are giving you 3 choices, one, refuse our treatment. You will be cordoned off in an area for those who wish to refuse treatment, along with your likelihood of exposure to Pathogen Six. This means high risk people who refuse treatment will be kept only with other high-risk people who refused treatment.

"If you wish to accept, you will be cordoned off in another area, but there are 2 choices here as well. One, indirect exposure only, or two, direct injections into your blood stream.

"It works like this, if you want the treatment to be indirect, you will be kept in a room with people who chose either indirect or direct exposure. If you want indirect, then it will only be in the environment. There may also be those who chose direct in there with you.

"Direct exposure means we will inject the virus directly into your blood stream, once per day. You will also be allowed to live in the indirect area, and thus be exposed in the same ways as those who want indirect exposure.

"If you change your mind after being allocated, let us know and we will attempt to relocate you. If you wish to stop receiving direct exposure, please inform us. If you wish to stop receiving indirect exposure, it is more difficult, but we can move you into another section of the station. If you initially chose no-exposure, but wish to receive it, you will be moved into an exposed section that fits your desired exposure and risk category.

"You will be in six different isolated sections. For those of you who are low risk, you will be in either section one for no exposure, two for indirect or direct exposure, and three for those who back down off of exposure. High risk will be given sections four, five, and six with the same pattern: four for no exposure, five for exposure, six for post exposure.

"To make sure you can make informed decisions; each section will be allowed to keep contact with all other sections at all times. That way you can keep informed on what each section is doing in relation to your own. We encourage you to keep an eye on the situation as it develops.

"We will begin moving people in three hours. You have that time to make your initial selection. Thank you."

I hung up the intercom and took a deep breath. The Ethics Board approved, but part of my inner scientist voice, said, "We are testing this on people, no control group, so if we make it worse, we may not know." Unless we found a way to make statistics work for us.

But I couldn't think of anything that would compensate for the lack of a control group. Or really a way it could be worse. Still, we could record as much data as possible.

"Do you think we can interview people; ask how they are doing as things go along?" I asked Diane. "I feel like we should try to figure out how well it works now as we won't be able to later."

"I know what you mean, but I am not sure we can do it now either," said Diane. "It is an emergency, both on the ground and up here. We may have no choice but to just go with our gut here."

She was right, although I still felt like we needed science behind us.

"Maybe we could use any of the previous infection sites," said Tone. "There are so many if we must have a control, we should use one of those. That and other failed treatments."

"That will do for me, if we have time for it," I said.

Eventually everyone signed up; almost everyone in the "High Risk" group wanted direct exposure, and the handful of people who didn't, wanted indirect exposure. So, we decided to cancel the three sections, and instead moved them into one larger section, where they would have more space.

The low-risk group was more difficult. About half wanted exposure and half didn't, so we did our best to move some things around, while wearing biohazard gear, so that everyone had room. We ended up using a temporary barrier to separate those who had been exposed from those who chose to not be exposed.

Then we did the first round of blood tests.

"The good news," said Tone over the intercom, "is that, thus far, all the blood tests from the low-risk group have come back negative. While it is too soon to be certain, it is possible you could still be OK in the end."

"The bad news is that some of those in the high-risk group have come back positive. While we all hope our virus plan will work, this is still troubling."

"Everyone in the high-risk group will be given a separate semi-quarantine area to prevent future spread."

"The other groups shall remain the same in the meantime. Keep in mind that it is possible that people in high-risk sections have not been exposed yet and are fine so please remain calm."

Then we began moving everyone who tested positive into the quarantine zone to care for them as best we could while we kept them separate from the healthy patients.

I looked up Dr. Fry. He was in section seven-- perfect.

"Dr. Fry do you have a minute?" I asked.

"Yes, I see you are doing well," he said, "What is it?"

"Could we use the quarantine zone, like the one I was kept in, as a way to allow people to transfer from high to low-risk?" I asked, "As in, if you pass that you can move on to low-risk?"

"I was going to ask you about it; I asked Soukup and he said to ask you," said Fry.

"You got a plan for it?" I asked.

"Yes, take a look?"

I looked through the document and gave him a nod.

"Ladies and gentlemen in the high-risk zone, we have decided to enact a plan to move some of you into the low-risk zone if we can. It will be a 3-day stint in the quarantine zone, during which you will continue to receive your chosen exposure setting in isolation. If there is no infection present after 3 days of tests, you will be released into the low-risk zone, either post exposure or continued exposure at your choosing."

"We will select people primarily by lottery, then occupational priority; anyone who is not already known to be infected with Pathogen Six will be allowed to enter the lottery if they so choose. The winners will be taken to isolation, if they show no sign of infection after 3 days they will be released into low risk. Otherwise, they must either stay in isolation, or return to high risk."

"There are only ten isolation rooms on this station, so we will only be able to take in that many at a time. We will work to convert more rooms if possible. Thank you for your patience and cooperation."

The next day, almost anyone in high risk who could, signed up for the lottery. We took the numbers and ten winners were chosen. Then we did the next round of blood tests.

No changes since the day before.

Then we gave everyone a survey, detailing how they felt, what they thought their chances were, and any symptoms of Pathogen Six they felt, plus an area at the bottom for any comments.

I also walked through the areas in a hazmat suit. It was different, as this station was a home away from home. It also seems like everything was fine... I knew it wasn't but I couldn't see the specter of death.

Three days in I made another walk through.

No signs of infection thus far in the main areas. Then I visited the hospital where those in isolation were kept. I walked through the walls between the rooms, and occasionally looked through a window when allowed. In the waiting area for those who wanted to move from high to low all seemed well.

Then I visited the infirmary where the patients were confirmed to have Pathogen Six. By this point the infection usually becomes visible with a persistent cough. A cough that was notably absent in all the patients in isolation. I surveyed them and while they looked miserable and complained about how they felt, they also seemed to be relatively healthy... it's a start.

This hypothesis was backed up by blood tests we ran later. Those in the infirmary were still sick but were not as badly infected as most people were by this point. Then some more results came in... good news.

"There is good news today." I said over the intercom hoping to cheer some people up. "There have been no infections in the low-risk area so we are assuming all people in the low-risk group are now perfectly safe as we are well into the time frame where symptoms are visible and all results have come back negative. So, if you are in the low-risk group, go celebrate. We hope to have you moving freely throughout all but the quarantined areas of the station very soon... congratulations."

As soon as we could, we made a clean pathway to zones one, two, and three. The moment it was open, people started running down the corridor. Diane was one of them and she found David, Olli, and Lady, who were all very happy to see her.

You know those videos of loved ones, you know, spouses and kids reuniting, or videos where a dog sees its human after a long time? Diane, David, Olli and Lady managed to tick off all the boxes. There was hugging, Lady was jumping and running circles around her family, tail going crazy. David even broke down in tears.

"It's... so good to see you again," said David.

"Hey. I am just glad you and Olli are ok," said Diane.

Frankly I probably would have been a puddle on the floor except the only family I brought on board was Robey. And he was in the high-risk zone, and a robot, so, it would be a few more days.

A day later and our first ten lottery winners had cleared and moved out of the quarantine chambers. And no new infections had popped up in high risk. But after a day of blood tests, I was given the duty to check up on those who were infected.

The first person I saw had a sore throat and a runny nose. No real cough, but they did say that breathing hurt. The second person, was pretty bad, with a nasty cough. The third just had the sniffles and was trying to convince us she was fine. They were all over the place but generally no worse than anyone else would be in this situation.

Then the blood tests for the rest of high risk revealed one more person to isolate. Well hopefully tomorrow would have no new news on that front. I met the person who we needed to isolate. He was the stereotypical macho tough guy, except for some silent tears.

"Well... do I really have it?" he asked.

"I am afraid so." I said, "Look, there is not much I can do other than promise to help. Your odds are better...

the other patients are developing slower. It's possible you might recover."

"Spare me the rest of your speech," said the man. "Just... don't get my hopes up... if I'm going to die let me at least see it coming."

"...Ok." I said before I escorted him to his room. A makeshift chamber thrown together by bots over a few days. Doctors worked in biohazard suits as no one trusted the tarp walls. And with occasional surveys tuning up Pathogen Six in the general area, the distrust was well placed.

The next day came and went, no new cases of Pathogen Six emerged.

"We will wait three more days," said Diane over the intercom. "If there is no change then everyone in high risk will be cleared, if there is a change, we will let you know. But this may be the end of the risk."

After another three days... it was done.

There were more celebrations and reunions and Roby managed to be as excited about my return as any dog. And one thing I wanted to check up on was one of our patients.

"Are you alright ma'am?" I asked through the speaker on the wall.

"Well (cough) I feel horrible," said the patient. "And I am on an oxygen mask... but... well I am still alive... aren't people usually dead by this point?"

"Usually," I said. "Without wanting to get your hopes up things might be turning for the better... at least in your case."

"What do you mean?" asked the patient.

"Your blood tests came back... no Pathogen Six... at all," I said. "They want to move you into better isolation... so that we might be better able to protect you from other patients. Do you think you can handle that?"

"I guess," said the patient and I helped move her into one of the real isolation chambers.

"You still ok in there?" I asked once she was moved.

"Maybe," she said in-between coughs.

"Ok... Hang tight; if you are still fine in three days, we will call you cured."

She nodded. If this is what we think it is... we might have a reliable treatment. Two had died... but we already had a full Isolation area.

The next day came... one more patient passed away... but we now had a waiting list for the proper isolation chamber. Half the remaining patients were ready. We lost three more patients over the next three days... but not only were the first group free and clear... but the rest were no longer infected. By this point there were twelve left. We moved ten into isolation and kept an eye on the remaining two.

I checked in... all of them were coughing like something awful but were still alive. The first ten patients had been moved into the main infirmary. They were also coughing up a storm. But with everyone alive. And then another three days went past and then, everyone was out of isolation.

Granted most were still in recovery but, well it made the mood celebratory… we had a weapon against Pathogen Six. There was cause to celebrate.

Tone however had a more somber expression than I did.

"My parents, they went to the hospital, they have it, Pathogen Six."

"Well, we have a cure," I said, "There is a chance we could…"

"I know," said Tone, "But I know we can't ask them to prioritize them, I mean, I wish we could but…"

"I know," I said, "Lots of people are sick. Still, maybe, we will be going after quarantine zones. There is a good chance they could be fine."

"If we rush things, we may make mistakes."

"We have to hurry anyway," I said, "And I think it is almost time to think about wider dispersal."

"How do we want to do that?" he asked. I didn't have an answer.

Chapter 11

Now for the final challenge: mass production. Our new virus, quickly named the Savior Virus, needed to be produced in large enough number that it could take hold quickly. To do this would require a large number of bio labs. Not impossible, after all gene therapy clinics were often converted to bio labs in order to eliminate genetic diseases and to treat other medical issues. There's certainly a lot of them, just one catch.

"So out of the five hundred or so bio labs across North America," began Tone, "Thirty or so are active. The rest have either been destroyed when a Pathogen Six outbreak occurred because of a failed experiment, or in a riot, or happened to be in an infected area, or have otherwise been abandoned."

"I checked Eurasia." said Diane "Nothing available."

I sighed. This was going to be a long day.

"I checked the orbital and lunar facilities," I began. "Most were designed for research, no mass development, and most have also been claimed for other important roles." One of the things the orbital and lunar cities needed from Earth was medicine.

"The good news," said Diane, "is that the Antarctic cities have some labs they would be willing to let us use. Most of them are even free of Pathogen Six. Bad news, most of them were also mothballed after the foundation of the Global Republic."

"So, century old tech that has been neglected for... 50 or so years," I said. "Not very helpful... If we could get some supplies to bring them up to date..."

"Not likely," said Diane, "It might be easier to build a new lab... or not... I don't know."

"I vote we visit one of these labs before deciding," said Tone. "We need all the help we can get."

Diane and I nodded and the next day we were leading a mission to one of those defunct labs.

I grew up in Antarctica for ten years before my parents separated and heard versions of the story of what the Antarctic Commonwealth was. In college I made it a point to find out the truth. It was a plutocracy, founded by wealthy individuals drilling for oil. Lots of people moved in to work jobs that might have been harsh by todays standards, but people were desperate and there were places, at the time, with worse working conditions. Twenty years later advances in fusion made oil obsolete, the Commonwealth couldn't switch to providing a different resource fast enough, lost favor internationally, became practically bankrupt, and was eventually forced to join the Global Republic as an "uncooperative territory."

When that happened a lot of its people looked around and decided they would rather live literally anywhere else, so they moved. People emigrated by the millions until the population fell to less than one million, on the entire continent. Most of the cities were quietly abandoned. Those who chose to stay relocated to a few settlements on the coast. The ones that still struggle are a shadow of their former selves, and often forgotten by the wider world.

Maitri City was one of many abandoned Antarctic cities. Most of the buildings were standing only because they had been preserved by the weather. Windows were smashed, walls covered in old graffiti. Its oil refineries stood empty, barely standing at all. A mine outside of town was boarded up, and cordoned off by a fence that was falling over. Its streets were vacant... a ghost town in every sense of the word.

The biohazard suits were usually on the warm side, today they were surprisingly cozy. Though I could hear the wind blowing there were no animals as this was too far south for seals and penguins. Most of the crew who came with us took samples to see if the area was free from Pathogen Six as we had believed. Tone, Diane, and I headed off for one of the Antarctic Bio labs. We arrived, pulled open its door, and walked inside.

It was a mess, Tone immediately walked over to an overturned desk frozen to the floor. He gave it a kick to confirm that it was indeed going nowhere. The door on the wall was on the floor, its hinges broken, I began to wonder if this place had anything for us.

"My guess is that this whole place was looted," said Diane.

I walked past the door into the main lab... and there was stuff here, old equipment.

"Slightly better in here."

Diane and Tone walked out to meet me.

180

"Why was this place not looted?" said Diane.

I walked over to a piece of old lab equipment and said "Because this thing was old fifty years ago. I grew up in places not so different from this. The Commonwealth spent fifty years slowly dying. If this lab's previous owners were lucky, they might have been able to occasionally cobble together new-ish equipment from spare parts from places that were upgrading to the latest and greatest. The looters probably decided it wasn't worth the trouble of picking it up."

"So... does it still work?" said Diane. "Does the building even have power or water?"

I flipped a light switch expecting the lights to stay off... and they did.

"No power," I began. "But..."

Then the lights turned on.

"... if we could... we have power?"

Diane walked over and hit the switch... the lights turned off... she hit the switch again and the lights turned on.

"Right." Said Diane, "how did that happen."

Then a lab technician ran in saying "Heads up we got the fuel cell... working... so..."

Tone grabbed his radio and held it in the air. "Use this next time."

"Ok," I said. "We have power, and we could use the electricity to melt water if we need it for anything."

"I suppose it is too much to hope for water to actually be working," said Diane.

"Yep, faucets frozen," said Tone turning some of the faucet knobs, "but we have a working building."

"To be fair we can probably find working buildings anywhere," said Diane. "Do we know what this equipment does... this looks a bit like a DNA printer."

"It is, it's an old model but I don't know if it still works, hang on." He ran off.

"What do you think?" asked Diane.

"It's isolated," I said, "if something goes wrong here, we will have time to fix it. And this equipment while old, might be able to handle some tasks to bolster production."

"Agreed," said Diane. "Though using equipment that is so old does bug me. Will it be able to work as well as we need it to, will it work at all?"

"If nothing else, this could be a good incubation site, and the lab's infrastructure probably is usable."

"Guys," said Tone over the radio. "I found the spare parts; the closet is fairly full. You could probably build another DNA printer with this."

"That's good," I said.

"Also, I saw the water pipes; they are intact, no damage. If the other facilities like this are in as good condition, this could be a boon for us."

"So, we can maybe use this?" I asked.

"I think so." said Tone.

Later that day we were back at Failsafe and...

"The results are good," I said. "No Pathogen Six, no Beta microbes... it's safe."

So began a large-scale revamping of that lab as many others were similarly checked out before being brought online.

It was about time too, the reports coming in from elsewhere were not good. If a place was relatively safe, there was a flood of refugees. Many of whom might be sick, and might have doomed entire communities. The plague was spreading like a wildfire, across people, across forests, across jungles, across grasslands; only deserts and tundra slowed the various alien pathogens. Even then it still progressed, advancing toward any human settlement. In orbit the various space station cities that existed were safer, but none of them could produce everything they needed themselves. The death toll was unknown, but most estimates put it at least half a billion.

"We can use this one as a testing ground," said Diane as we began setting up. "We will sort out the issues here and now."

"What... oh right." I said coming back to reality.

It made sense to me, as I tried to figure out how we would man it. The lab had no robots, and those where few and far between at the time. Even if we did, I doubt we would find anything compatible with the old equipment.

As we were setting up, another shuttle suddenly stopped by. I didn't recognize the dark-skinned woman, until she spoke, she was Zabia Sall.

"We hear you needed more man power," she said, "I found some volunteers."

I looked at the people behind her, a full shuttle of people in military uniforms, some of which seemed to fit somewhat awkwardly on the wearer. Then I noticed lights in the sky that looked like more shuttles coming in for a landing.

"Ok..." I said, "Um... We have lots to do so... let's get started."

Tone, Diane, and I relayed our instructions to the volunteers, most of whom were military. What they lacked in training with the equipment they made up for in following instructions to the letter, and sheer dedication. Once we figured out what we needed them to be doing they would do it... no questions other than requests for clarifications, no complaints unless we left them with nothing to do for more than a few minutes. Credit where it's due... this might have been impossible without them.

After three days our little lab was working and we had some Savior Virus. Mostly we had been incubating it and having it produced at Failsafe. But we had produced quite a lot of it.

Our next step was, well... I visited another lab, one in the center of a hot zone in Eurasia, close to Singapore.

Nothing was alive for miles, no bird song, no living plants, no insects. This was Beta microbe territory now, as far as I knew, the place I was in might as well be dead.

Beta microbes had taken over... but the lab was pristine. Local authorities promised it was on the grid, I checked the power and it was working... so that helped.

I examined the lab... everything was in working order. I went back to the shuttle that landed me here, and grabbed a canister holding Savior in solution. I then moved the canister into the lab and set it off. It began spraying an aerosolized solution of water filled to the brim with Savior Virus. While the virus had a suicide gene to keep it from going too crazy, it would have more than enough time to get a foot hold here. And with a few more canisters dotted around the area… it would be clear in no time…. I hoped. We then went back to Failsafe for full decontamination.

Over the next five days I flew back to that lab and several more labs. Then it was safe to fly people in.

"You will wear a biohazard suit when there," said Soukup. "No exceptions, not even once."

"Ok." I said, "Um will everyone else have one?"

"We're down to letting people have them based only on need," said Soukup. "We will do what we can for the volunteers but not everyone will be able to get the best protection. And right now, you are someone we need alive. So, no matter what, keep the suit on… no heroic taking it off to help boost morale."

"Has this been a problem?" I asked.

"No… and I intend to keep it that way."

I nodded. Then I boarded a shuttle which dropped me off at the lab I was going to oversee.

As I arrived another shuttle pulled up and dropped off about thirty volunteers. None had proper biohazard suits, some didn't have anything at all. I felt awkward wearing mine.

"Ok, so let's get started." I said before giving them their assigned tasks. On the first day we refurbished the lab, on the second day, production started. It was then that one of the people without a suit started coughing.

"Are you ok?" I asked, worried that she was infected.

"No," she said, "But don't worry… I just want to stop my children from being infected… they are all I have left and it is already too late for me."

"You think you're infected?"

"Not Pathogen Six." She said "Cancer, normally it would have been a minor treatment, but with things the way they are."

"Do you want me to put in a request for priority treatment?"

"No, I have time, besides I have children, they are near Auckland, and right now there is a massive outbreak…"

She tripped, "Sorry, not as strong as I used to be, but as long as I am of some use...."

"What's your name?" I asked, helping her up.

"Lei," she said.

"As soon as this is over I will put in a request for you to get help... ok?"

Lei nodded.

Our first batch was finished, and another shuttle stopped by to deposit the finished canisters at the end of our day. They were off to cities on the edge of the infection, and to more labs in the hot zones. One week passed and I was testing samples.

"Negative," I said, smiling. "If this means what I think it means, we have controlled it."

Soon enough the data was ready.

"That's significant," I said, "We have controlled it."

Tone was smiling.

"No, we haven't controlled it," said Diane, smiling even more than Tone.

"Um what?" I said, the smile falling from my face.

"If we were controlling it, I would have expected more positives," said Diane. "I misread the manifest earlier. This was further into an infected area than I thought. And if I adjust the data for that..."

Another significant result showed up.

Diane clapped. "We haven't just controlled it... we have beaten it back." Her smile grew, "This is not containment, this is victory."

Then there was cheering and hugging.

One week later I was on Earth again. This time without my suit.

One week ago, this was an infected zone... today it was safe. The fence around the town was being disassembled. While the plants were often still dead or dying, the mood seemed almost like a party. I looked over and saw Lei hugging two kids... they looked just like her.

Things were actually going okay. We had stopped the spread of Pathogen Six and in a few places even beaten it back. For the first time in ages, I felt like things were looking up.

Then I got a call from Soukup.

"Hello," I said, "Avery here."

"Hi," said Soukup, "Are you sitting down?"

"Um... No... Should I be?" I asked, looking around.

"Yes... please find a seat," he said.

I found one and sat down, took a deep breath, and braced myself for the inevitable bad news that comes after 'are you sitting down?'

"What is it?" I asked, "I'm ready."

"Your mother passed away from Pathogen Six two days ago," said Soukup. "She was volunteering at one of the refurbished labs when she got infected. We would have told you earlier but... you were kind of busy."

"I... well... thanks... for informing me I guess, but..." I said, between stammers.

"Do you need tomorrow off?" asked Soukup. "We can probably live without you for a day... and you might need one."

"I... I don't... yes," I said. "Just let me know if you need me for anything."

"I will," said Soukup, "Take care of yourself, all right?"

"Understood... Bye," I said.

I then tried to find my way back to the shuttle. It was scheduled to go back into orbit soon anyway. I was tired and I felt like I had been hit in the chest. Two days might have been enough to save her. Normally people chattered in the shuttle, I kept quiet.

After the shuttle docked at Failsafe, I walked back to my quarters. I tried to take my mind off things. I wanted to take my mind as far away from here as possible. Somehow, I ended up watching the news.

"So, in good news for a change," said Eric Long, "The GHA has announced that the Savior Virus has actually allowed them to beat back Pathogen Six and they believe that the end is in sight as more facilities are expected to produce more of the virus over the next few weeks. Though many warn that this is not over."

A politician identified as Shurti Sakkara spoke in another portion of the screen.

"While the end of Pathogen Six appears imminent, rationing will continue for the foreseeable future. We have estimated that it is possible that we could distribute enough food to keep everyone alive until all of the farms are back in full swing. I urge the people of the Global Republic to remain calm and work with us. We are facing a tough year ahead, but if we work together, we can hold the Global Republic together. We are not out of the woods yet... but we can see the exit."

"Some wonder if the government is ready to handle this event," said Long, "Is it?"

"We made many contingency plans," said Sakkara. "As evidenced by the existence of Failsafe Station, we knew that an event like this one might occur. We will have to make tough calls, no doubt about that, but if we can survive the next year, then we will likely recover in time."

"And if we don't?" asked Long, "What if the government falls? We have already seen the return of disease... are famine and war next?"

"Maybe," said Sakkara before a small smile. "But we defeated famine and war once before... and if we have to, we can and will defeat them again. I would like to thank the research teams on Failsafe Station for their tireless work... as well as our military forces who responded in our attempts to keep order and slow the spread of Pathogen Six, and of course the countless civilian volunteers, many of whom sacrificed their lives in an attempt to control and stop the spread of Pathogen Six. Thanks to their efforts, everyone else has a chance."

"Thank you for your time Sakkara," said Long.

Long then turned to the camera.

"We attempted to get Dr. Hutton on air but his boss, Dr. Soukup, claimed that he was too busy with his current responsibilities. As for everyone else, stay safe."

I spent the next couple of days quietly mourning. I wasn't part of the celebrations.

Eventually I got back to work and, well, the Savior Virus went exponential on us. Over the next month it wiped out Pathogen Six, then, as we had programed it with a suicide gene and with no hosts to infect, the savior virus disappeared.

Next year I was back in Houston, doing something that I hadn't done in a year. Getting dinner on a Friday with Diane and Tone.

"Now I know that I would normally say don't worry about the price, but this time, if we cannot go too crazy?" asked Diane. "A lot of food is still expensive."

"If I can have something that isn't kudzu or algal crackers, I will do what I can to keep it cheap."

"Chicken, fish, tofu and insect protein are available," said Diane. "I am mostly worried about one of you trying to order a steak or pork chops."

"That's assuming they actually have steak or pork chops," I said. "Most restaurants don't have beef or pork anymore."

"Next year maybe?" said Diane. "Then we can come back and each have a steak, you know, when the worst cuts don't cost four hundred dollars."

"Will that be happening?" I asked. "I mean, yes, I would like to."

"Yes, it will, I don't care that you're off to be the new Secretary of Public Health next week, or that Tone is going to take part in the official investigation, or that I am going to be in Tokyo to teach biology at a top school. We. Will. Find. Time." said Diane.

Tone and I just looked at her, then at each other, then we shrugged.

"Maybe I will pay next year," I said.

"Maybe." said Diane, "Just be sure to be here." She said, "Or in New York, or Nairobi, or maybe visit me in Tokyo. Doesn't matter, we can decide later."

So, we got to the important business of searching through the menus. About half of the items were crossed out. Of what remained, half involved kudzu, algal crackers or insect protein, but they did have a fried chicken sandwich available with a side of fries so I had that. Tone went with a tofu burger, and Diane went with grilled catfish.

"I got an email from someone I worked with in the producing Savior virus phase." I said "Lei."

"She the one who has cancer?" asked Diane.

"Had, …she got the treatment last week and is cancer free now."

"That's a relief." said Diane. "Survived the unexpected plague of doom, but then died to a normal cancer, that would be just sad."

I nodded "Without the cure it is deadly, we just kind of forgot that."

"In the death total... did they count people who died of ordinary diseases?" asked Tone.

"I think that the two point one billion did count them," said Diane. "No one was keeping good records as things deteriorated, so we may not know exactly; they just counted the people missing."

"How are they going to do the memorial?" I asked.

"I think that each city will build its own," said Tone. "One for everyone who died would be too big."

Our food came shortly thereafter and we enjoyed the first good meal together in a year. New jobs, new life, it felt like the disaster was finally over.

Acknowledgments

To my Mother for her support.

To My Aunt Jane Zacha, and My friends Shannon Garrick and Lin for proof reading

To Ezra Rendleman for designing the cover.

Members of the Carolina Forest Authors club including but not limited to.

Ann Jefferies, Ellin Weesel, and, Debra Colletti

And to you for reading this

Made in the USA
Columbia, SC
27 January 2022